THE MERE FUTURE

Sarah Schulman

THE MERE FUTURE

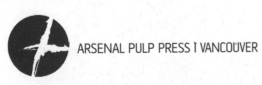

ARSENAL PULP PRESS I VANCOUVER

THE MERE FUTURE
Copyright © 2009 by Sarah Schulman

ARSENAL PULP PRESS
Suite 200, 341 Water Street
Vancouver, BC
Canada V6B 1B8
arsenalpulp.com

This is a work of fiction. Any resemblance of characters to persons either living or deceased is purely coincidental.

Book design by Shyla Seller
Cover and interior image copyright © Alex Lukas
Photograph of Sarah Schulman by Nayland Blake

Printed and bound in Canada on FSC-certified paper

Library and Archives Canada Cataloguing in Publication:

Schulman, Sarah, 1958-
     The mere future / Sarah Schulman.

ISBN 978-1-55152-257-9 (bound).–ISBN 978-1-55152-266-1 (pbk.)

     I. Title.

PS3569.C5393 M47 2009   813'.54   C2009-900857-2

For Kathy Danger
Special thanks to David Bergman

Sacred knowledge, in the hands of fools, destroys.
—The Upanishads

1. COMA TOAST

(IN THE FUTURE, when things are slightly better because there has been a big change.)

Back in the present, my lover Nadine and I have moved to a new part of town to reaffirm our vows. The old streets were too familiar, telegraphing past failures and complaints. Each landmark, a bitter nostalgia.

We'd come to that time in our romance where we knew too much, and so the real loving could begin. Deception ends then, the deception that one is more important than the other.

Now for the new regime:

1. communication
2. negotiation
3. reconciliation
4. healing

This is the sequence of a strife worth living.

To forgive pain is to create a friend for life. To be silly in such a moment, viciously wrong, is to create an enemy. If you are cruel and stupid when you should listen and be kind, don't blame her.

Look at me, Reader.

I don't believe in closure, I believe in the reopening of love.

People can get court orders to keep communication from happening, why can't we get court orders to sit down and talk it through? That would be my idea of a better world.

Amazingly, and wonderfully, I do live in a better world. You see, the society that surrounds my feelings has finally taken a huge step forward, one that can inspire me to do the same. For now, some days hence, Our Town's most recent election has yielded the most surprising victory. At last, voting has created progress and just as I have become emotionally up to the task of betterment, my government leads the way with:

THE SELECTION OF OUR NEW MAYOR AND HER MARVELOUS WORLD VIEW

Yes, the citizens have chosen visionary change at last! Who knew that New Yorkers would some day wise up? But now that they have, I can too. Finally, all hopeful gestures can reach their desired goals. It's The New Era, and just because we all decided to try something true.

I'm excited about this. And proud of you.

Evidence reveals that facing and dealing with problems requires more than one person with a spine. If only one person has a spine, it will be broken by the other's lack. But two spines, two capacities for recognition, and two evolving individuals with their own specific knowledge—this is the formula for shifting to the freshest spot.

New Yorkers have collectively agreed to change for the better, and so have "we." Nadine and me.

My society inspires us, and I am happy.

Tomorrow morning we exist, coexist, form habits, and exercise comforts in Terrainville, a new Manhattan neighborhood next to Flower Market.

The elevator in this building is made exclusively of ice. So, to rise to each occasion, the tenants must drink great quantities of gin until we think that we're better off than we are. That's how we get in and out of the apartment.

Delusion, sedation, unwarranted jubilation, warranted.

Gourmet soup and little chocolates decorate our refrigerator door, photographs of home-made meals. We, so busy, only have time to make coffee, trying to chit-chat in the mornings between long periods of sludge. That moment, to say what I did and hear what she will, that brief loving presence after a night of shared sleep, that is the true time. All the rest of the day I fear and regret, so I can share a coffee with the girl I adore. I never even make toast. The joy of being with her lets hunger play a vague second fiddle.

But, just as the greatest pleasure complements fear, I also refuse to own a toaster. I fear that the bread crumbs will attract mice, thereby rendering our home sordid and a disgrace. An excuse for rupture. I'd rather forgo shame than have toast. The specter of crumbs on the floor, or burning bits of bread. Those flames would leap, and make all my dreams disappear. There are, after all, live gas jets buried historically behind the light fixtures of these old, landmarked hovels. That's what makes this apartment so desirable, that it has a dangerous past. Substandard living conditions are hard to find these days. They're edgy and give the tenant special status, as I must daily avoid combustion to keep my love drinking coffee before me. Take no chance. One little fire and that would be the end of me and all my labors. All my little bits of beauty. For this reason, I occasionally buy toast on the street, even though I always overpay. And then fear all day.

Ours is a busy neighborhood. There are many outlets for toast. Some are dank and some are dreary. Some are exclusive. Some whistle for me.

One morning, before work, when none was said nor done, we slid in with the sun and then slurped down the stairs for togetherness and toast. The rain on the plate glass window, umbrellas, and one unrecognized smiling devil in a see-saw of gray passed by. We looked at that figure, crossed our legs, and flapped our shoes. Ah, togetherness.

Turning slyly, I gazed at Nadine's humanity over the rock-hard table. In Los Angeles, people earn money and cover their kitchen counters with pink granite. But in New York City, no one has kitchen counters, we slice on ingenious contraptions that fit our little space. So, the only rocks in our apartments used to be in our hands. Reminders of the protests of our youth. Their outcomes can be most easily spotted in contemporary commerce. Hence, with some satisfaction, I glanced outside at the Unisex Sari Shoppe Imported From Chicago, and then turned back quickly, just in time to notice two new truths about my light, Nadine.

1. Over these years, she has changed so much for the better.

Blessedly, I have loved her long enough to notice. It would have been stupid to hang up the phone and never see each other again.

2. She now has grey hair.

Neither of these "facts" had ever been that way before. And so I had consequently to ask myself the following question:

Do I have grey hair too?

In the past, I would have feared this kind of associative inquiry because it would have been a reflection of the narcissism at the base of my homosexuality. The other should not associate to the self. Or so they say. All my life I've worried about being selfish, about listening, about considering the other, and so I've been repeatedly crushed. Then I realized one sunny day that true narcissists never ask themselves these questions. They destroy arbitrarily and never pay the price. Now that I am free of the fear that I might be narcissistic, I am plagued by the fear that you (Reader) truly are.

Natural disasters and historical traumas provide the opportunity to bring people together. But there is nothing as divisive as human cruelty.

Definition: The consequences of your actions on others do not matter = Cruelty

That's how I know I have truly lived. I fear the unaccountable ones. I already know the damages that they do. The only mystery remaining is, are their ranks about to be swelled by (Reader) you?

Only the fear of being a selfish homosexual has been quelled. This relief, to now be able to associate with others without feeling pathological about it opens up all portals. For I was then able, at that Brekfsto-Resto, to ask the real question, the one at the heart of the manor.
    Are all women going grey?
    Or is it just me? I mean her?
    You can spot the ones who dye it. Every strand is the same hue, or so deliberately varied that the viewer is distracted from the necessity of aging. The bad dye job looks stinky. What's the point? We all know what's under there. I prefer Nadine's natural variety, the streaky kind. I like a body that reflects someone's life. But that's the thing with us gray-haired ladies (if I am one), some of us have very girlish bodies. Robust and hungry. We are animals. Our hair is irrelevant except for aesthetics (huge). Hair color means nothing

about our potency, everything about our history. We've risen and splattered, risen and splat. We know what it takes to land flat on our backs. We should be honored. Walk among us, serve us tea, and look deeply into our eyes. I like our guise, the truth, the sad vulnerability of knowing. Of not hoping any longer for what can never be. Of loving the things we do privately.

This toast with Nadine was a casually loving date between two old cronies, two members of the same secret society who had formed one of our own. We'd signed the card in the ancient days when you could phone up any other gay girl in the United States of America and she'd call you right back. Sadly, now that we're freer, no one returns phone calls unless there is something in it for them. But my gal and I reminisce fondly about the former tribal bond and are much the better for it, even though you can't stop the future. And why would anyone want to try? That's the thing about my group. Lesbians have a great shelf life. We don't need plastic surgery. The rest of the world runs around trying to grab hold of some younger person's tale, while we get more beautiful every year. Our knowledge becomes rarer and more alluring.

This morning I would be disorganized, late, wrong clothes, unbrushed. Nadine glided from the ice room with a fashionable scarf around that prominent neck and a soft impeccably clean sweater. It showed off more of her body than there actually was. *Oh my*, I thought, feeling like a devil. Brand new shoes on her, dainty black boots. The leather not yet creased, its life before it. Buckles hinting tastefully at bondage. .

I took a new look at my old love. If her eyes had been bluer, they wouldn't have faded away. Maybe I could have seen through them into her heart. Her mouth? Can't remember. Instead I was riveted by the attention she paid to her knife. I was jealous of the butter. Then, connecting again, a few dirty thoughts were allowed to pass across the toasty table. Knowing that hesitancy is mature, I thereby felt insecure. Aroused, aware, and recommitting. We have to preserve what is lost in order to know that we have lived. But if it is lost, it cannot be preserved. So "loss" is the wrong word. The thing remembered is being seized by absence, and so I must, must, must grab it back ... Oh yeah, I looked down right then and saw a long, black silk blouse, oodles of tactiles. Real tweeds. Heels.

Do you grasp the moment? Two knowing lovers with a chance for more in a better world. What a place to start a futuristic story. Looking to the future means there will be one, which is a sign of great hope. And so, optimistically, we go forth.

Dark skies mellowed, shook, and died. Now, pools of dried butter in crispy whole wheat, we departed into the former rain and she went along with kisses on the sidewalk. Although no longer illegal, still crusted with the frisson of potential humiliation by others. Two well-dressed women in love in the splurge of middle age.

The lighting was so demure, naturally gray and smoky. We have had better lives, after all, than we would have being straight, but only together. Alone is the fall. Into their mercy. And they don't have any. The others. Nadine, it's our mercy or none.

I have a collection of memories, too numerous to list, or even to hold conceptually, too onerous to miss, mutinous too.

. Brandy in snifters, like actors drink in the magazines Nadine works for. Actors. They're everywhere. Especially on the advertising pages my dear one produces with electronic/digital/solar/oceanic systems that seventeen individuals used to be paid to do. Only some of those folks have found new jobs. Others are now too rich to work, and the rest? I forget.

Our shared knowledge has brought me through every scary moment.

We've each pleased more women than any United Nations agency. After all, only the crazy can resist shutting their eyes and getting fucked, despite the lost loves gone poison, intentionally. I don't believe in breakups. If you look and listen, every loving moment can be praised.

Hey you? Still here? Yoo-hoo.

Give me your body with full confidence. I'll know what to do. Then, very proper, a nice kiss goodbye. Once again we did each other a favor.

The street is always gorgeous afternoons after making love. I've known that feeling since I was seventeen years old. You can't remember it, just recapture it.

When Nadine comes home tonight, I'll be lying between the sheets waiting for her to melt the ice in the lock.

Manhattan wasn't always this way.

2. SPOON

I HAVE ALWAYS believed in precision. That it is, in fact, the center-
piece of truth. The continually vague are continually lying. Try to
pin them down and they'll slash out like wolves.

Like most of this era's cerebral women, I work as a copywriter.
Boiling it all down to a few words. This job is about reducing experience to bite-sized morsels, which is generally dehumanizing and
yet requires humanity. You have to notice the truth in order to be
able to avoid it. In the olden times I would have been a great corporate secretary, bringing a woman's touch to a big bad machine. Now
they don't have secretaries anymore, just vice-presidents. These are
the saddest men I have ever seen.

I've been at this job for the rest of my life. At some point long after my adolescence, every company that could survive merged into
one … with distinct divisions … so downsizing … while never-end-
ing … no longer seemed to be happening. It was economic mitosis,
an undetectable action of the natural world requiring a microscope
to observe. We were blinded by the fun of all having the same boss,
THE MEDIA HUB, while our units provided Identity. Everyone
knows what their friends are going through when there is only one
field. Empathy becomes easier to muster.

When I finished my Postdoctoral Studies in Placemats of the
Moyen Age, I took my place at THE MEDIA HUB. It was waiting
for me. On my first day of work in this branch, so long ago, I went
to the corner and took a sauna. In those times, before things were
slightly better, even waitresses needed to be able to translate from
the French in order to get a job. Everything was so competitive

then, even being exploited was hard to get. All women had to be overqualified to earn a basic check.

In that particular sauna were two old ladies, Eastern European accents, recent émigrés. This was decades ago now, before Bulgarians became the world's street people. The new white underclass. Currently, Albanian junkies hook on every corner of the western world. And Japan. But this was before their fall from Pseudo-Socialism.

I looked at my ancient naked colleagues and saw that one, talking about her grandson's bar mitzvah, had a number on her arm. Just like my old granny's cousin, who I met for two hours in an airport café. The tattoo on my cousin, Dora, began with the same letter as the tattoo on the flabby arm of this naked woman in the tub. The letter A. For Auschwitz. Dora had been a slave laborer there, working in a munitions factory. After the war, she was dumped from the Displaced Persons' camp to Israel, where the authorities considered it work experience and gave her a job in a munitions factory.

"My cousin was in the same camp," I said conversationally, reclining against the jacuzzi's caress. "Auschwitz."

"I was in Auschwitz," she said. "But how did you know?"

"The letter A," I said.

"That doesn't mean Auschwitz. It means *Arbeiter*. Worker. I was a slave."

"My cousin too," I congenially assured.

"Then she should get her money. They're paying now, for the work. I got a check from Volkswagen."

Her name was Frieda Berger. She had come from Romania ten years before. She was nice, friendly. Sad that my cousin had recently died. And later I thought—*this is the importance of precise detail.*

You see, I could have gone through my entire life from my soft seat of comfort believing that A=Auschwitz, that prisoners were identified by their locale. And all my life I would have been wrong, and somewhat deluded, thinking that geography mattered, when actually these people were identified by function. Not knowing this information would have made me miss the whole thing. How dehumanization actually works. And in my armchair of generalized thinking, this other person's life would have remained so fuzzy that its reality would have been unknowable to me, while I thought I knew it all. I wanted to change history in order to make me feel safer, and the lack of precision would have let me do it.

I report this to you with hindsight.

Now, as my own city is changing within me, every moment filled with telling detail, I know that I have to really pay attention. Now I live in the midst of a huge social transformation, and those can always go either way. Sometimes, come the Revolution, we all eat strawberries and cream. Sometimes, come the Revolution, we only eat strawberries and cream. What if you don't like strawberries and cream? Sometimes, come the Revolution, we *have* to eat strawberries and cream.

Nadine and I watched our new beloved Mayor, Sophinisba Breckinridge, rise to power. And then we watched the changes that followed. Until, one day, the changes actually affected us. This was that day.

This very revolutionary strawberry and cream morning, I received a notice beckoning me to a meeting with one of America's most powerful cultural arbiters: Harrison Bond.

"Mister Harrison Bond requests a personal audience with

you, as a consequence of the great social change that is currently underway."

I had been chosen, suddenly, somehow, to have the opportunity to meet with him and taste the schlag. Wow.

That's the new system, I thought with the grandiosity of recognition. *The new system is working for me.*

I, a lowly copywriter with great secret dreams, had been selected by the New Order for individual attention. This was true Democracy, finally. Anyone can get inside the system now. It's all random, as it should be.

You see, it had finally been acknowledged that there was no relationship between merit and reward. That while on occasion people doing truly meaningful acts were given presents, it wasn't because they deserved them. It was a coincidence. They got the presents because their fathers went to some college, or they had sex with an ugly casting director, or they made the person in power feel good about their own mediocrity—some coincidence like that. At the same time, it seems that the vast majority of truly valuable gestures—the kinds that expand understanding and create hope— were excluded from recognition. So, since those with experience, praise, and stature were found to have no merit, and the truly deserving were so alienated they couldn't invest in any system, the only fair solution was to just open the floodgates and let everyone in. Hopefully, it would all sort itself out.

Once the standards had changed, the doorways to opportunity were suddenly filled with feet. My big dawgs included. It was a grand chance, but I had to keep track of all the details in case I blew it. Then, at least, I would have a true story. To tell Nadine. And we could muse, dissect, and laugh. Regardless of the outcome, right? That's love, isn't it? — having someone willing to share the disappointment.

At The Opium Restaurant on Avenue F, the moon recalled those of June and other months with transitional weather. It passed, hovered, came too close, and then recoiled. The citizens found this confusing: the seduction followed by withholding. But then, they each remembered the last woman they loved, and the moon's ride suddenly felt familiar.

Movement, unpredictability, seasonal containment, and public transformation without public transportation. A lunar borderline personality disorder. The shifting sky assured the existence of fate, divine order, external consequences while waiting endlessly for the broken-down bus.

At the corner bus stop with no bus in sight, the doomed waiters glanced into The Opium out of boredom and hunger. But they had to be in another world, awaiting their ride. Later, perhaps, one of them could grab a stand-up hummus at Mamoun's Falafel. But those not on the go, the most jejune of our clan, sit here and demurely lunch as I wait for the tall, quasi-presentable man.

A spreading cloud darkens the restaurant's front yard and then dazzles it. When the shade finally passes, only the shadow of my now-arrived companion looms brightly over the table. Mister Bond. Young man, not so young, whose fate has been sealed by his own physicality. This meal, a symbolic truce between two worlds, The Mediocre and The Small, was mandated by the sudden, shocking social advances of only one year before. It all stemmed from Sophinisba's new decree, the *Dissolving the Pretension That Has Come to Define Literature Act*. It was the nine-hundredth campaign promise that she'd actually kept.

My co-eater, Harrison Bond, had been an important figure in the dominant paradigm due to his persistently relative youth and persuasive lack of life experience. He practiced a kind of literature called "Modern Situations." Each story involved a couple, a prosperous but banal location, and breezy journalistic sentences. The couple would have glib, ironic experiences. It was a conceit that diminished life, his power. But, in this pause between hope and ancient distrust, I poured us the wine. *Chateau du Lait.* It's the post-raw years now, when this pour took place. Wine comes from Nebraska. Those abandoned crystal meth labs turned out to be good for something. Smoked mozzarella is made in Detroit in former automotive plants. Ford mozzarella or Chevrolet. The poor are still poor while the working class smokes mozzarella for their daily bread.

As I watched Mister Bond silently chew, I began to reflect on the miracle of our changing collective life. Now, by the luck of the mighty pendulum, one less person goes hungry under our cherished new system because I hand over my lunch to a passing collection truck every other Thursday. We took a vote in Manhattan, each man, woman, and child. Would we rather that people go hungry OR would we each give up lunch once every fifteen days? We voted to share. And for that same reason, so that I can get my reasonable due, this tall fellow has to endure a lower stature than he always expected to enjoy. This new system was devised by a German Jew (Sophinisba's mother's maiden name was Rosenbaum).

Life is only a shiver. The light through neighboring Coke bottles is a lonely sign of impure sensibility. Everything else on our plates is natural and home-grown. We can sit out in front and eat peacefully now that the homeless are no longer banging through our garbage cans. They're busy eating my lunch.

We waste in peace.

Ah, social tranquility. Thanks to Sophinisba and her Retrocrat Party, things are a little more hopeful than they once were. So no dirty claws lift old rice from garbage cans to their own cracked lips. No rotten scraps interrupt our lovely meal. No resentment from faces other than our own. No one else's hunger.

3. NEW LIFE

NADINE AND I both voted for Sophinisba. The other choices were: Milando Spenokovich on the Catholic Resumption Party, Jena Chelsea Gore III on the Celebutante with Education Party, Boo-Boo on the Party Party, and Eileen Myles on the Seniors for Seniority Party. Sophinisba won us over with her slogan:

"Conceptualize Beyond Your Task"

It swayed us.

Usually, Nadine voted for the liberal guy, and I voted for any black person who was not conflicted about abortion rights. I figured that they would be the most reliable. And they were. But they never won. Yet we united politically around Sophinisba Breckinridge, who made us feel both safe and invigorated. She was a former social worker from the days when there used to be social services. That was quaint and endearing. She had never been beautiful, also reassuring. She had big, intelligent ideas, persuasive in their precision. And then, it happened. We went to sleep, and when we woke up, she was the mayor.

Surprisingly, Sophinisba started to do everything that she had said she would do. This was unbelievable and difficult to grasp. All New Yorkers walked around stunned. Eyes opened, backs straight, flabbergasted. More people could fit into the subway because we were all so erect. And after the first week, the whole world started to notice. When you change New York, the universe burps. Someone had kept their word.

I try to keep my word.

If I say, "I'll have that for you by Wednesday at three o'clock," then I'll have it for you by Wednesday at three o'clock. What always defeats me is when people promise Wednesday but really mean a year from April. Can't they just say so in the first place? Should I second-guess that they're lying, or just believe people and get hurt? The answer? Believe! I have to. I couldn't live another day if I didn't think that you would keep your word. Once said, it must be done. Life falls apart when we waste our precious dream time trying to diagnose in order to avoid being misled.

So, personally, Sophinisba impressed me. Though I didn't completely register the precision of her quest. *Precision*, that word again. It reappears because truth was again involved.

After wondering together, Nadine and I went hand in hand to meet old Soph and talk to her, face to face. That's how she spent her first month in office. Around-the-clock coffee and rugelach with each of her citizens. Mayor B asked questions and answered them, urging us all to take another bite. Women always have more power when they bring some food to the table. Lulled, Nadine and I basked in Sophinisba's smile from under the brim of her silly, endearing hat. All her tricks were humanizing, made us relax, this lack of fashion sense. The ugly shoes. Dull hair.

Her first question was:

"What are you ladies thinking about?"

"Paint," Nadine answered. "I work in front of a digital-squigital all day long, and long for something more tactile than screens." She sighed, open-hearted, telling her long longing to her sympathetic government. "Sometimes I want to leave technology behind and return to the days of hands, materials, smells."

"I see," Sophinisba said, rugelach dust on her widening lap. "It's more individual, is that it?"

"Oh you," Nadine cooed. Swooning as though it was someone fuckable, charming, and needy, instead of an astute Mayor with a bad perm.

"I'm asking myself what a city is," I said, following Nadine's trusting example, and also scampering for attention. "I've lived in this one all my life and its meaning it still too big to grasp."

"Maybe it's unknowable," Sophinisba wavered, allowing doubt to be a legitimate perk of human governance. "Do you love your city?"

"I love it."

"Me too," she sipped conspiratorially.

Yes, we both loved the same unknowable living mass of flesh, steel, disappointment, possibility, and that patch of sky whenever one looks up.

"Why, Ms Mayor?" Nadine was being openly flirtatious now, which was interesting to watch. "Why do you love it?"

"Because," she said. "Here we are, fragile beauties in the same tender space. We are surrounded by magnificence and the capacity for great evil. We share this duality, in front of each other, with our weak enticing bodies. That's what it is to live in a city. And to love it. There is one thing every human being needs, and I think we all know what that is."

We nodded.

Not another sound clamored to be heard. We knew what word she was referring to. We knew what that one need was.

Satiated, we left and another wide-eyed neighbor took our place.

Nadine and I wrapped around each other, soft within ourselves as only the protected can be. This was new and great. Considering that most people have a very hard time thinking, it is advantageous for our common overlap known as *society* to be both smarter than the masses AND a force for personal serenity.

"Conformity is unavoidable," Nadine whispered in my shell-pink ear, "so anyone who raises the standard to which most will conform, well, that chick is gesturing towards joy."

Agreed. And what I loved most about Sophinisba was that her philosophical approach had a material application. She figured out morality and then made it real. And the reality of our common New Yorker vulnerability translated into the one word, the word so obvious that Sophinisba didn't even need to utter it. That word was ...

HOMES

Sophinisba knew, as all city dwellers come to understand, that nothing good can happen between fellow citizens—no program, no idea, no change, no hope, no chance—if people do not have a home.

"Everyone must have a home or else there is no nation," she announced the next day. "It would be a joke."

I felt the jangle of keys in my pocket and realized that soundtrack was the heartbeat of the healthy soul. Without homes there is nothing else we can do for each other that works. Once Sophinisba let that cat out of the bag, more changes got made. Pronto.

When the headlines started, they never stopped. In one month she built so much low-income housing that the real estate market crashed. People who had overpaid at least had a nice place to live for the rest of their lives, and the speculators got what they deserved.

It just stopped making sense to buy something for any reason other than to live in it, and that was fine with me. Plus there was plenty of construction work to go around.

Nadine came home from work one night announcing that anyone who wanted an apartment could find one. And they weren't these huge impersonal prison blocks, all the same putrid brick. No, every building was a different size. They had stores. They had backyards, and porches. They were different colors. Suddenly prices made sense. A six-floor walkup tenement with mice and no closets was no longer three thousand dollars a month. People were only willing to pay what it was really worth, and so that place rented for eighty-five bucks. A studio apartment with a kitchenette hovered between fifty and sixty dollars. And if you had a family of six and needed four bedrooms, then rents came up to two hundred.

The transformative consequence on New York City life was immediate and complete. The impossible burden was lifted from people's skulls. They didn't have to worry about being out on the street. Outside was no longer a threat of potential disaster. Now, folks who had been killing each other because of proximity could each move out and get their own place. People lived together because they wanted to see each other's gorgeous faces in the morning. They wanted to continue the great conversation around-the-clock.

"How do you feel?" I asked.

Nadine and I looked each other up and down.

"We still belong together," she said. "Even though we could each afford our own bathroom now, I want to share one with you."

There was more joy and acknowledgement in my little life. And people with kids could finally make noise when they had sex, because their new apartments were large enough. No one had to devote their precious soul to gathering rent. They could go to the park or take a walk. Time was not money anymore. Time was just time. It was as if the streets opened up before us. The city was shared now, not partitioned. We could offer each other more. And so we looked at each other differently, with more compassion and interest. Home became more comfortable and therefore more important. People were not trapped in their apartments.

This is what happens when the pretending stops. When someone goes through life with their eyes wide open. And when that someone is allowed enough power to act on what they know. That's it! That's what we City Dwellers have achieved for ourselves! We've allowed someone to think and then we allowed them to carry out their revelation. We allowed things to get better. This made us love ourselves even more, and created more opportunity for even more change.

No one was that shocked when Sophinisba's next step was to seal off four boroughs and declare us an Independent Protectorate. Staten Island was made a part of Texas. No one actually knew what an Independent Protectorate was, so it was exciting to be something new. And we didn't care at all what the rest of the country thought. They've always resented us for our good looks, so no love lost there.

Her first act as an Independent Protector, on a Monday, was to institute a minimum annual wage of forty-five thousand dollars a year. That meant that every single person could go to the dentist, have a vacation, and save up for a dream. On Tuesday she established a maximum annual wage of 100 million dollars a year. The common wisdom on the street was that no one person needed more than a hundred million dollars a year, and for those who made more than the limit, the leftover went to prop up the rest.

From then on, when we stepped on the bus in the morning,

each one of us paid proportionally. If women earned seventy-five percent of what men earned, we only paid seventy-five cents, while they paid a dollar. WOW. It was the dawning of Reality-Based Conditions. Each according to their ability, each according to their need. Life was filled with recognition. Finally.

Then, she banned all franchises.

Everyday on the way home from work, Nadine and I saw the world revolve. New Yorkers are fast; within a week, each shop in the city was the idea of a particular individual person and their friends. The shop owner could have it be any color and choose their own interior design or absence of it. The quality varied, the items were not pre-selected. *Starbucks* became a euphemism for *Tyrannosaurus rex*. Consistency was no longer considered desirable. In fact, it became icky and weird. Prices were original and low, because of the sane rents. Get it?

Immediately, every single life was improved. It was spectacular. We all had homes. We all had commerce that resembled the strangeness of our individual organisms. Daily life in our beloved city was more personal, and so the Retrograde Party meteor of the Old Era came to an end with the Era itself.

Now, daily life was kind of a compulsion, one worthy of feelings high and low. Provisional periodic poverty is fine for the character, just not deprivation. Who needs it? For, despite the unavoidable complexities of love and loss, redefining how we think about Home and Store had tremendously improved our moral plight. Having better values and lower rents leaves the concerns of death and sex their justified place. They are no longer eclipsed by falsely imposed problems like lack of shelter and other unnecessary pain.

In the glow of this communal light, Nadine whispered into my neck.

"You know what's worrying me?"

"Did I do something wrong?"

"No," she said. "It's not you. It's Sophinisba."

"Yeah." I smiled serenely at the mention of her name.

"I have a big question about her."

"What is it?"

"How is Sophinisba paying for all of this?"

"Hmmmm?" I felt a nostalgic kind of unease.

"You're not listening to me," Nadine squealed.

Shocked at the accusation, I leapt from my deceived serenity with shame, pain, the desire to truly make amends, the courage to change. I looked her in those gorgeous eyes. I mustered every ounce of determination and conviction. I never wanted to be selfish, it wasn't the real me. It was the disease talking. I truly loved, and that was the ideal that should guide my actions if I was ever to be a fully integrated human bean.

"Must be something in the private sector, I think," I said, carefully.

Nadine smiled back, distractedly, and I hoped the transgression had healed. I was delusional. Nothing heals in one moment. It needs tending. Cutting corners festers the soul. And so the path to hell was laid. How could I know that this problem of my callous dismissal of financing would soon determine the future of my heart?

4. BOND

BACK AT THE Opium Restaurant, Harrison Bond was a very private man, and yet I knew so many things about him.

Before THE CHANGE, he was primarily known as the author of the novel of the year, *My Sperm*. John Updike, late chief critic for *The Brand New York*, had said that Bond was "one of the brightest young stars in the literary universe." He used the word *panoply*. He said that Bond was "the new Cheever, the new Mailer, the new Pynchon, Roth, and J.D. Salinger. And, oh yeah …Toni Morrison."

Bond had a quiet, troubled sadness. He wore an extra-large baseball cap on backward. He'd once had a pierced ear. He stayed in a chair and liked to read. He was bald, had gone to prep-school, was brave enough to have had adult braces. He dated actresses, even two at once. He suffered from depression and was rich. But sad. He felt put-upon, and yet bore the responsibility of his talent. He whined. He wielded power behind the scenes and everyone knew it. He was struggling with his alcoholism, and frequented *the rooms* on occasion, especially the AA meetings with other sad celebrities, and then they'd go out for coffee and try to keep hidden away from fans. He had written many articles for expensive magazines. One was on designer cell phones, one was on fennel. So, when he ordered three Bombay and tonics, I wondered if this was a product of his swollen liver or swollen bank account(s). Doesn't all gin taste the same? Yet, being so private, I couldn't ask him a thing, since his allure worked wonders.

Here is the opening paragraph of *My Sperm* by Harrison Bond:

Thompson Ward had a quiet, troubled sadness. He pushed back his baseball cap, scratched the scar where his pierce used to be, and knocked back another Bombay and tonic, swearing it would be the last one of the day.

I am not my sperm, he thought. And then poured himself a double.

I had actually read the first two paragraphs of *My Sperm*. It was about a young, tall man who was found to be the last fertile man on earth. And yet, being private and somewhat sad, a bit of a drinker, he was not satisfied. He never knew if women actually liked him, even with his slightly monstrous seven-foot frame. Or if they just flattered him for his sperm. It was made into a movie, a television series, and finally a Broadway musical. Financially, Harrison Bond was set for life. People would always remember something about his literary wad, and he was guaranteed permanent aura. And yet, he was somewhat sad.

Now, because of the miraculous social shift achieved by Sophinisba and her folks, this depressed wealthy icon was forced to speak to me. It was odd, this obligation. What would happen?

"As you might know ..." He cleared his throat. Harrison feared sounding like his father, the golf pro. He loathed his father, but secretly followed golf. He loathed any recognition of his own authority because it forced him to be benevolent, when, after all, he felt like crying and wanted someone to take care of him. "Do you know?"

"Know what?" I asked.

Already our dynamic was quite complex.

"Well, Miss Weigert, you do know that I am the new *Brand* editor, uhm ... I mean, the fiction editor of *The Brand New York*."

"No, I didn't know."

"Oh."

"I mean ..." I wanted him to like me. But why? "I don't know who the old editor was either."

"Why not?"

"I only read *The Brand New York* when my girlfriend Nadine drags me to competitive yoga meets. I sneak a peek at her copy between asanas. I never understood its organization. It seemed to be something for people who used designer cell phones and ate organic fennel. You know, I'm a copywriter. I don't wear alpaca socks."

"So ..." Bond trailed off, burdened. He didn't know what to do now. My answer had, unwittingly, made him terribly sad and insecure, and I felt terrible about it. I became worried for him, and desperately wanted to take care of him. How did that happen? It was miraculous.

"So?" I prompted softly.

"So, since I'm new, I have new ideas, which will be different, since I am different," he whimpered.

"Is that where I fit in?" I had been wondering about my fit. Not knowing what Harrison wanted was one of life's less voluptuous experiences. Panic ensued. I knew the odds were likely that I was about to do the wrong thing. But what would be right? What? What? My mind skidded on the icy freeway of fear. I was doomed, doomed, by my own lack of *savoir faire*.

If I was a Buddhist, I could look at this fellow and think that only loving, only knowing matter. Because Buddhism is the occult pastime of our age, I could understand that few grasp the experiences I've lived and that this was my blessing. And vicey-versy. I could come to terms with the slow pace that invades the depth of my soul when I truly love, when I truly want to understand. But every time

I try to be a Buddhist, I fail, simply by trying. I sit in rooms with people who have not yet achieved their goals. They say that the best way to achieve your goals is not to try. But their lives are not proof of that theory. It seems obvious, the contradiction. You have to try. I don't mind washing water, but can't I still want a glass to drink out of? Panic, panic, breathe, breathe. Accept that what others do to me is the punishment I deserve?

Or, I could seize the momentito.

Bond.

He held up that week's issue of *The Brand New York*. The cover advertisement was for Red Snapper Douche. *What a great piece of graphic design*, I thought, associating directly to Nadine, my own personal fish, my dearest delish, and her workplace struggles, occurring simultaneously with mine. How romantic.

Politics had changed so, these last few months. Now that housing was under control, and small business seemed to thrive, there was a group turn to focus on our jobs as the next place to change the world. Let people rearrange their relationship to the machine. But now that the means of production is mental, there are no burly iron workers of yore. Labor is intimate, between us and our computers. Individually, we may each try to subvert, but, of course, individually in the long-term can't change much. We each have that one computer that we stare at and grow to love/hate. The illusion is that it's personal, that it loves us back. In the end, we produce smarter, edgier products, and the structure of employment remains intact. THE MEDIA HUB is the major unit of social enforcement; was it going to be the mommy we never had, or a prison of measured time? And what is the difference?

In this dyasma, my sweetheart Nadine was employed by THE

MEDIA HUB, as were eighty percent of citizens who had jobs, including me. She dreamed of being a painter while living chained to software. This contradiction between The Wish and The Real inspired her commitment of conscience towards the DeMarketing Movement, a spiritual state that had no material reality. It lived in the minds of workers as a hope, a virtual opposition. No one ever did anything but think about it, but somehow the thought was comforting. It was Tdzen. The knowledge that another life was possible—and may actually be happening simultaneously without our knowledge—but acting to achieve it was socially strange, and so we occasionally yearned while struggling to accept the necessity of amnesia. We read about our yearnings in the *Daily Oprah Report*. And then they caught on. Yet sometimes, in the dead of night, Nadine wakes up suddenly and realizes that marketing has taken over yet another corner of her soul. She whispers this to me, shudders, and makes me proud of her sharp, useless perceptions.

But, here, sitting before Harrison Bond, hype was such a seductive crutch. And visions of his red snapper slapped onto my plate.

Engage the snapper or refuse all fish. These were my choices.

When Ralph Waldo Emerson went to visit Emily Dickenson's brother next door, she stayed home.

Why?

My guess?

She knew he would humiliate her.

What slimy, scaly thing was Mister Bond about to propose?

I realized in advance that I could never win, and yet still I hoped. How mortal.

I side with sinners and am recalcitrant. Bad strategy. But, on the spiritual side, writing is my art form, and so I know what dudes like this are doing. That's what makes his spectacle so difficult to disengorge. I work in white heat, halfway between grace and recognition. God must exist in order to be hidden. There is truth beyond theme, an art even in Mr Bond. Oh decisions, decision. Finally, I took my Power in my Hand and went against the World. 'Twas not so much as David had, But I was twice as bold.

"That's a lovely douche you have there on the cover of your magazine," I said quietly. "Is there an accompanying QVC?"

He smiled.

The deal was done. My submission confirmed. Now we could proceed.

"So, Missy," Bond said over his late-night breakfast. "I did a tincture on the cyberscam." He was eating wood-burned scrambled tofu with organic chanterelles, soy cheese, red chard, blackened Cajun fiddleheads, butterwheat focaccia toast with one-hundred percent real-fruit kiwi butter, green chili, organic red potatoes steamed in mock apple cider, and a side of turkey-arugula sausage cake. To drink, he had wheatgrass nectar with ginger and a fourth Bombay and tonic.

"Yes?"

He was nervous, poor lad, and my heart involuntarily went out to him again.

"Because of the new way of doing things around here, that we're all getting used to, you know … the changes …"

I nodded.

"I thought it might be symbolic to give credit where credit is due."

My cue.

"Oh you," I coo.

You've got to flirt with men in power, even if they know you're gay, even if you don't do it well. There is simply no alternative, unless you can age beyond them, in which case they can project "maternal" or let you be smart.

"We fed the range of human emotion into the Melancthagraph, and it revealed that the thing people need most in this moment in history is for a Punished, Deserving, Overlooked Person to be finally recognized. Research shows that this public reconciliation with the Previously Ignored will serve as a symbolic catharsis that will put all unrecognized people at ease and make them think that the new system could serve them too. Hope will be restored. Like actually knowing someone who wins the Lottery. It makes everyone feel that at any moment they may find a way out. So …"

I was suspended as fate pulled my chain.

"So we singled out the most obscure, unknown, best artist in New York City, and we would like you to profile her for the BNY."

"Me?"

"You're a slogan writer."

"Yes …"

"Who best to sum up an artist's life?"

"Okay."

I was stunned. I had always wanted to do something important and be noticed, then included. Could that moment be now? Oh, Dolly Lama, bless Sophinisba B.

"Our selected subject is quirky and complex."

"Great."

"You have eight words."

"Okay."

"That's the spirit," he smirked, happily content. "Here's the address. Her name is Glick. Go get her limbs and bring them back in your teeth."

With that he drained his glass. And cried.

5. PRE-KILL

ON THE WAY to the interview, I practiced my journalistic technique by asking myself a few interesting questions.

1. Am I trapped where I want to be?
2. How now, Tao Jones?

And finally, the most important and impudent of all:

3. What are little girls made of?

Road crews were taking down billboards, and any kind of brand name or mass-reproduced symbol was being quietly painted over. No more Nike swooshes, no more yellow arches. It was visually a whole lot quieter out there, but also more complex. I could no longer just glance at a sign and know what it wanted me to do. I had to really look at it. Each one had its own code. Walking down the street took more time, if you were a curious person. And the repair crews weren't wearing uniforms. Everyone and everything seemed to be a civilian. Civilianization had a new look.

I was excited. Nadine practically swooned, it was mass art direction from the bottom up. Oh, the tremor of glamor. Could I really be on the path to a new light? This could happen, as well as that. And that! Opportunity had knockers. Maybe I could end up as someone special.

As soon as I began to imagine myself as a person deserving of love, instead of just happy to have it, Bond's face loomed over me as that of a VERY GREAT MAN. Since he could never help me before, he had never mattered. Now that there was the promise of "help," he mattered a lot. Before, I did not ever think about him; if his name flashed in front of me I blipped. But now, his potential benevolence situated him centerfield of my consciousness. Now, I cared about him. I became worried over him. Suddenly, I realized, I was now terrified of a man I had previously ignored. The effort to make him less powerful had actually made him ever so much more so. Now there was so much that he could take away from me that I had never had in the past.

The nightmarish imaginings of possible future deprivations were unending. I'd spend hours thinking of what I might never have unless Bond said okay. And you know what? I discovered that to be afraid of losing something that you never actually wanted is a very humiliating experience. If I didn't suck up to this angle-headed glibster, I would not be able to be glamorous, as I now wanted to be. I would not be able to earn the living that Nadine and I had never imagined. The funds that would enable my true love to get away from the keyboard and smear paint instead. I also had some desires on my own behalf that I was too ashamed to articulate.

I passed a bonfire of shirts with advertisements on them, logos and pictures of dumb products that were fattening and tasted bad. People had decorated their bodies with these items for years and never asked why. They had never asked why Tommy Hilfiger didn't have to pay them to advertise his business on their chests, nor had they ever wondered how they had been convinced to pay Tommy Hilfiger instead. Well, that weirdness had come to an end. From now on clothes would have designs and colors or any words the wearer had thought of themselves. They could also be plain white. The people tending the fire were relaxed. They could have been anyone, and so then could I.

"What's happening now?" I asked. "Have all the big chains gone out of business?"

"Nope," a sloppy, quiet guy muttered, tending his ashes. "Just out of public view. They're still gonna be bigger than ever. We just will have nicer things to look at when walking down the street. We won't always be reminded."

Invisible chain stores or invisible chains?

Another Sophinisba innovation. One suited to aesthetic principles.

Now I could answer my own question.

Was I trapped where I wanted to be?

The answer? *Not yet. But maybe soon.*

I wanted to be trapped in a life where I called the shots. Where if I said, *"Should we wait for a subway or take a cab?* is a question about race and class," it would be okay.

Tao Jones went up three points.

And little girls are socially constructed, so they are made out of our minds.

Committed to improving, I began to accept my newly required tasks. I would have to start reading all those boring writers like Harrison Bond, actually finish their books. I would have to remember their derivative and limp "ideas" so that I could care about them. I would have to follow *The Brand New York* like baseball, see who got traded, who was a star. I would have to study the terrain so that I could rise to the top. And once there, stay close to my enemies, watch their every move.

Yuch.

I panicked.

I didn't want to take in information that I don't want. It's the insistent extra. Horror finding me. Horrifying me.

Why was Bond doing this?

I felt trapped by progressive change.

Wait! Accusing Bond of conspiracy was giving him too much credit. Lets face it, the sad truth was that ... co-optation theory might be happening to me at last.

These were my realizations in the eerie light of the flaming logo'd shirts:

One of two things would happen. Either I would prove myself to Bond, he would let me in, and I would become like him. Or he would throw me one bone and then toss me away.

With this new knowledge, I arrived at Glick's house.

6. THE MOST UNKNOWN ARTIST

GLICK'S ADDRESS, 123 Siege Street, was situated on a block I did not know, about a half mile from Old Ixtapa, just to the right of North Chelsea. This was a quiet neighborhood of Manhattan, filled with chicken bones. The residents entered the houses through ancient bodegas and then crossed interior courtyards with a hint of apple blossom and Old Gold.

On the stoop there was a painting standing in for the former door. A man's body had been painted over and over so many times that it had congealed into two green squares floating on top of some limb-like black. Then I got closer and found something very surprising. The black passing as both profile and background was actually filled with passion. The canvas cried out "Molest me!" so I put my hands all over it. What could have led me to act so inappropriately? To become so messy?

Then … it happened. I had a revelation about life from the sequential foundation of a work of visual art. The order of feeling was revealed to me:

hope light fear confusion lie
hope light fear cowardice destruction
hope light fear courage resolution

The person who lived in this house never gave up.

WOW, I could not wait to tell Nadine about this. And then, the real revelation occurred. It was about Nadine herself. That SHE was what made this excitement all worthwhile in the first place. Because I could share it with her. If I had no one to tell it to, what would be the purpose of living it? What was the point to learning how to love if there is no one to love? Then I understood Glick's tragedy. She had learned how to love but had no place to enact her understanding except this sticky outdoor painting welcoming nonexistent guests to her nonexistent front door. It was the art of loneliness.

After all, if a person wasn't lonely, why would they ever make art? They could just be with Nadine instead.

And then I rang the bell.

"*What a sad surprise,*" the bell sang to me. "*How unexpected. I wanted it to be different and so I've waited patiently for so long, with no reason. I waited for something better, but only missed out on fully realizing more of the same. Ding Dong.*"

It was that kind of doorbell you only press once.

I guessed that Glick was some kind of eccentric. It made sense. As my friend Michi Barall says, "Alienation creates eccentrics and revolutionaries," which are not, after all, the same thing. Her out-of-it-ness was obvious from the state of her front door. That was a fate I wanted desperately to avoid. Also, being considered by others to be a crackpot was out of the question. I've never been stable, so I don't need stability. I don't need safety, I've never been safe. But strength is a necessity for the strong.

"Come in," she said, standing in the doorway, blocking my way. And there you have it.

Glick stared and stared until I finally took responsibility and pushed her aside so that I could follow her command. Then we sat down on mismatched kitchen chairs. The interview had begun.

It was clear from the start that she was a typical old-fashioned artist from the Old-Fashioned School. The kind Nadine dreamed of joining. She was not conceptual, digital, aerospacial, or architectonic. She was not botanographical, electrictronicfecal, or Inter-D. Glick used paint. All her books had smudges on them. The refrigerator was covered in blue fingerprints. Every single article of clothing in her doorless closet had white paint smears. There was paint in her hair, and it had always been there. Her walls were one big abstract smudge.

I checked my notes.

"What do we owe you?" My first question.

"You owe me ..." Glick fell out of contact. She hadn't thought about compensation in so long, her fantasy had expired from lack of use.

"What do WE owe YOU?" I tried to emphasize, snap her into it.

Glick looked up, her pale grey eyes clouded swamps. Her skin, sagging and pasty, her nails bitten, her hair like abandoned steel wool. Her veins, her ragged forgotten nails. "You owe me ..." And again she faltered.

"What?" I shouted "WHAT?" I got much closer, tried to move energetically, smile, and sparkle—anything to wake her up. "What do WE owe YOU?"

"You owe me ..." She coughed phlegm into a crusty old brush cloth. "You owe me *radical heterosexuality*."

"What is *radical heterosexuality*?" It sounded vaguely familiar, yet meaningless. Like *People's Court*.

Invigorated by the elixir of someone paying attention, her eyes boinked open. Attention was the tin man's oil can, fresh raw meat on a rusty soul.

"You owe me … THE VULVA!" She yelled, and its propulsion knocked over her chair. Glick sat on the oilcloth covered floor now, her legs out before her, her bottom dangerously near a pool of turpentine. "You owe me … REPRESENTATION. You owe me …" She fell back on the floor. Exhausted. And then suddenly popped up again, fully revived. "YOU OWE ME A LIVING!"

Shocked, Glick blinked. Then, robotically, she dragged out some old scrapbooks and showed me photographs from her distant past. They seemed like more primitive versions of the kind of pseudo-neo-arty advertisements designed by graphics students who had studied Nan Goldin and Audrey Hepburn, and then photoshopped them both on the same day. These pictures were quaint. They were naturally distressed, cockeyed, and overexposed. As if by accident. There were young people looking old, instead of the other way around. These authentically young adults all wore some strange version of Gap clothes, but each one's outfit was slightly different, off-kilter. Like the photographs. There was a feeling about these photographs that was very strange to see, it tingled in the back of my neck, and then I recognized it from some very ancient memory. These people were … ugh … sincere.

"It's all here," she said, pointing at her heart. "That which I was. That which I did."

Next she showed me photographs of happenings, performances, and plays from the past. Live people being watched without screens or projections. Just standing there. I guess they were Art Shows. Frankly, they looked like jokes. Like parodies of Political Correctness, that sort of thing. I was seeing the originals of some phenomena that had only been satirized, but never preserved. It was impossible to look at it without irony. The soul of this memory could not be engaged with a straight face. It was like bell-bottoms, or Peace.

"Excessive form and suggestive content," she muttered. Then Glick turned off the lights and hauled out a loud and creaky old movie projector, the kind that only turns up these days as a reconstituted planter. She actually projected a Super-8 film onto her smudgy walls. It was weird. I had never seen anything projected with a light coming from behind me before. With monitor screens, the light comes right at you. It's an entirely other engagement. With a film, you have to want to watch it. There is a way out, not a monitor standing directly in your path. It's a choice. Weird.

This particular one looked like a video clip except that it was out of focus. It had these painstakingly slow renditions of effects that nowadays are achievable in less than a second with a computer. But I think she had to spend weird laborious lonely hours achieving them in airless isolation with dangerous chemicals and creaky machines.

"I have a quiet yearning for tenderness," she said. "And that would be fulfilling." Then she looked to see if I had written that down.

"I'm recording it on my watch," I assured her. And she didn't know what to say.

When the film ended, the lights came back on and she handed me a framed, paint-stained photo of a group of friends, all young, with their arms around each other. They all looked different. They were each wearing different clothes. It felt psychotic.

"Where are they now?" That was Glick speaking.

"Yeah, where are they?" That was me.

"Mad at each other and me, or dead or stupid or boring or too depressed, too pathetic, or defeated, out of ideas, delusional, or bitter. Afraid." Then she scrunched her forehead. "Wait! I just remembered. This one is rich and slick and therefore equally out of reach."

I looked at the face of the only one who made it. He knew the secret of straddling opposing universes. He was a winner. How did he do it?

"I forgot I ever knew him," she said. "Personally, I have never sold a piece."

That seemed impossible. Everyone wants to buy something.

"Is it because you think it would be bourgeois?"

This was a sentence I had picked up along the way. Over and over again we were reminded that the reason people were excluded was because they wanted to be. They looked down on those who were in. They thought it would be bourgeois to be recognized and happy, so they purposefully kept themselves from enjoying what the generous winners so wisely chose to enjoy. I had been told over and over in so many ways that people like Glick loved being alone.

Glick looked confused and then laughed insanely.

"Is that what THEY are telling you these days? That I chose obscurity?"

"Yes."

"What a lie." She gnashed her silly teeth. "No way."

"Really?"

"No!" She couldn't believe it. "I have never sold a piece because I have never figured out how to shmooze. I just always said whatever I thought was true. WHAT A MISTAKE! Do you know how to shmooze? You're young. Can you teach me? It might not be too late."

"You'll never be able to do it," I said, without thinking. It was so obvious. "You're not user-friendly. You're too needy. You have no social currency. You're a freak. Without a normative side, you can't get in. That's it. Sorry."

I felt a special kind of satisfaction, because I was just about to be let into the world of the special, by Mr Harrison Bond. That's how I knew for a fact that she never would.

"But," she whined. "I have a personal momentum of ideas."

"Like what?" I felt sorry for this dork. Being user-friendly had nothing to do with ideas. "I'll try to squeeze them into eight words."

"Like the flesh and bone of cities."

All I could do was stare with astonishment at her ineptitude. Immediately, to protect myself, I assessed the differences between us so that that gap would never be bridged. Those differences would keep me from ever turning into That.

Don't get me wrong, I liked her paintings. In some ways they were overwhelming me with feeling, feeling so strong that I couldn't get up and leave. But they were feelings about Loss, about the Irretrievable, and the Lack of Justice. Those feelings were not in demand. Forget about them.

"Do you have a boyfriend?" I asked. Why did I ask that? To keep her even further away. I knew that she didn't have a boyfriend, and I wanted to reinscribe her failure.

"Oh," she said, minisculely. "You know."

"No, huh?"

"Well, while I do need to have sex to realize my passions, an actual relationship is ultimately too ephemeral for me. I'm too ambitious. I want my passions to last."

"Ambitious?"

"My ambitions are greater than yours," she glared, recovered. She started smoking and eating garlic.

This startled me. *Ambitions?* No one with ambition would ever act, look, think, dress, speak, or smell this way. How could she realistically expect advancement when Glick did everything wrong? I knew what I was talking about, after all. I was just about to achieve my subconscious career ambitions by following Harrison Bond's orders. She wasn't following his orders. I was. And I was also achieving my emotional ambitions by talking to Nadine while loving her. Doing both at the same time. Glick was loving and talking to no one. I was soon to be a complete person, while Glick would never, ever matter.

"People are so vague and unreliable," she said, speaking unknowingly about herself. "My ambition is for them to be reliable. My ambition is to offer and be accepted. I mean, I'd rather show a man my vagina than have him find it. I am so ambitious that my breasts are a threatening piece of industrial machinery. My ambitious sympathies lie with the lonely. What could be more desirous than that? I stake all on the intuitive character of thought. By presenting my obsession, I've humanized it. If you dig a hole, you need something to hold back the earth. I've got that something. My obsession. See?"

"But ..."

Confused, I smoked my first cigarette in thirteen years and coughed.

"Look," I said, astounded by her lack of perception about other people. "Pure abstraction is not appropriate to our time. People cannot interpret. Analysis is a drag. Abstraction, nowadays, keeps people from seeing the real and so feeds their baser, crueler instincts. Or else it is so real that it is too much to bear."

Then I really thought about what I had just said, and realized that I was about to realize something from which I would never be able to return, something that would fuck up all my dreams. This could not be.

Deliberately, I stood—took in the failure of will standing before me. I realized that I must never speak to her again. I had to forget that this way of living/thinking/looking/feeling was an option. It only leads to pain.

"Do you want some coffee?" she said, trying to remind me that she was a human being and had thirst.

Before capitulating, I ran out of there. I did not want to know yet another thing that would make my life harder. Even if it was true. I wanted to be like Harrison Bond. On top of the world, The World. I did not want to turn that corner.

7. THE UNKNOWN MASTERPIECE
by Honoré de Balzac

THE PAINTING ON Glick's door haunted me. But it intrigued Nadine, who asked for its description over and over until I realized that she only wanted the gestures of hands squeezing paint and didn't need the words. One night she photoshopped what she fantasized the door to look like, but it wasn't even close. Then, two nights later, she murmured in her sleep, "Glick. Glick."

I worked night and day on my article, when I wasn't working at work. In my research, I discovered that Glick's door was in the tradition of a visual idea first expressed, surprisingly, in a work of nineteenth-century French realism by Honoré de Balzac. He wrote it more than a century before painters discovered Abstract Expressionism. Weird, huh? That a writer could think of a painting before the painters could.

Amazingly, dear Reader, in a kind of event that can only take place in fiction, it was this very story, "The Unknown Masterpiece" by Honoré de Balzac, which Harrison Bond was reading alone, in his fictionalized apartment, at exactly the same moment. Like me, he had turned to Balzac because of a personal quest. Whereas my goal was to understand the origins of the idea of abstraction, Bond wished to conquer the word *like*.

The word had been bothering him quietly for some time, but his disgust grew cumulative, and finally he wanted to be done with it forever. *Why use?* he thought, in the fragmented way that people actually think. *What's the point?* he thought, in the more conventional and less naturalistic way. And so he decided to turn to a great master to find out how Balzac had avoided the mundane comparative.

Harrison was sick of *like* because even he knew that a metaphor must be natural to have true meaning. To compare one image to another is only valuable if you wish the second image to illuminate the first. To simply repeat the same knowledge twice doesn't do anyone any good.

As Harrison read this translation of Balzac, he imposed some strange uses of the word *like* to see how it felt. This is how a writer reads from time to time. One text exists on top of the other. Unless they are just trying to fall asleep.

Inside Bond's apartment, *a tree fell like falling leaves*. That could be interesting.

Inside Balzac's story, however, it was a cold December morning in France. A young man paced on the sidewalk *like* a husband about to visit his first mistress. *Sidewalk* is a modern word to convey the meaning of the side of a Paris street many years ago, don't take it literally, with contemporary eyes. The dusty rubble that pedestrians clung to while they dodged the flying shit of horses was all that was available to them. Our man climbed the stairs to his master's house, *like* a young mistress worried about the King's welcome.

If one compares fragile emotions, nothing so resembles love as the youthful passion of an artist beginning the luscious torment of his destiny of glory and sadness, audacity and shame, vague beliefs and discouraging certainties.

Would Balzac's young unknown's real talent lose itself in the practice of his art making, *like* a pretty woman loses herself in the wiles of coquetry?

As the story's poor neophyte hero stood on the landing greeting his teacher, he perceived something diabolical about the old man with a lace collar. The *maître's* forehead was bald, bombed, predominant, fallen, filthy, and on top of a smashed nose. This *maître's* thoughts had crushed both his soul and his body.

The *maître* beckoned the young'un through the threshold and let him into his first MASTER ARTIST'S STUDIO, his first smell of the Master's paint and his first sight of materials chosen with that acquired instinct of specific understanding and knowledge.

Before the boy stood a huge canvas holding three strokes of white. The day could not illuminate all the piece's angles, *like* fragments of torsos or a silver leather bag lovingly polished by a century of orgasms. Many years of those orgasms were self-provided, but then that became futile because the Master could no longer recall real-life sex acts in which he had actually participated with another person. They were too long in the past and too overshadowed by socialized emotions, that is to say, feelings about others. Because the *maître* could not remember, he could not believe that it would come to him again, and that lack of faith made fantasy impossible. Sexual fantasy implied hope. He had no hope. He had painting. That was all he had. The young fellow thought he saw the projected memory of an aureole that, decades back, had been offered to the Master's mouth with real love, but by now it had desiccated.

"Do you *like* it?" the Master asked.

The year was 1612.

8. THE LESSON

HARRISON BOND PUT down this book. It was a lesson he would never forget. He had started out trying to read technically, but then he had gotten so lost in the telling of the story that he forgot to look out for mechanics. That was the sign of a great work. Sadly, Harrison faced facts. No one would ever feel that way about *My Sperm*.

Bond knew that a person who could make him forget his self-consciousness must know something about life, and so he resolved to take Balzac's discovery to heart.

What Bond had learned was: He wanted never to become the lonely old Master. He did not want to be the wishful neophyte with all that suffering before him. So far, he had avoided both those fates. He was a *young* Master. If he slid even one step back, they would do a revisionism and decide that he no longer mattered. He would never climb back on. So that slide could NOT take place. The facts were in. Bond had to stay on top.

Loneliness was Harrison's enemy, like imminent cancer waving hello from every cigarette. He had to be very, very vigilant. Once you get Loneliness, it never goes away permanently. It always lurks and threatens to re-approach.

Right now he had a classically marketable personal conundrum that both deflected loneliness and provided good material. He was in love with two women and would soon have to choose. Bond checked his watch. He'd have to choose in three months.

Who were these two women? What were their attributes?

Well, each of them owned a television set.

Ginette had a color set with remote mind control, satellite, cable, and airborne. It had fifty-thousand channels. It had VCR, DVD, digital, laser, and molecular attachments. She could watch live or archivally, and she could also watch shows that hadn't been broadcast yet. Whenever Harrison was at Ginette's house, they lay in bed together eating Madagascarian take-out food, giggling in the soft shag and vinyl cushions, and watching future programming from Utah, Maui, and Taipei. It was fun.

The other love, Claire, had a small black-and-white box. It was vintage, displaying her eccentricities. There were five snowy channels showing programs from the 1960s. These programs were: *The Defenders, Flip Wilson, The Smothers Brothers, Playhouse Ninety,* and *I Love Lucy.* Apparently these were all that anyone actually needs. The two lovers would stretch out on the hand-made quilt and eat cheese and crackers and drink Fresca and giggle.

Whichever woman he chose, that was the set that he would be watching. He could live without the comfort and hip knowledge of the color/mind remote/nuclear set, and he could live without the bohemian currency of having something fetishistically in the know, but he could not live without the giggling.

Claire, the black-and-white girl, had soft luxuriant breasts with musty nipples, *like* perfectly warmed stewed apples. If he chose her, the day would inevitably come when he would no longer be fixated on her breasts and would then turn to the TV. That would mean night after night of marveling at the superiority of the past. A weird proposition for a creator of contemporary culture.

Ginette's breasts were not as intoxicating, but her living room was sexier. Ultimately, it provided many provocations to fuck. And when sex wore off, he could spend a lot time just changing the channels.

How to make this decision?

These were his true feelings. Did that make him a bad person? After all, he admitted it. Wasn't that enough?

In many ways, the question before Harrison came down to this:

If he could easily find yet another girlfriend as soon as the sweetness wore off, he would chose Claire and her black and white. But if the threat of age was soon to be upon him, and his desire/ability to attract would suddenly tatter like yesterday's newspaper, he'd better choose Ginette—the lass with comfy designer cushions. The wrong decision could be fatal. How to maximize and judge?

Harrison had fallen in love many times before. He knew what love was. Ultimately, each of the many women he had fallen in love with, he had loved with the same sincerity, fear, ardor, and detachment. Frankly, he had not loved a single one of them more than any other. He was familiar with love. In a way, it was not special. It was essential, regular, sublime like the morning, and equally available. It was not, and it was snot. Could he be deceiving himself, or perhaps he was just lucky? Would his luck continue? If he was just lucky, why had this goodness befallen him? Was he going to get away with life?

He knew that escaping punishment made him despicable in the minds of many, not the least of all—Feminists. The gross dullards of the planet. But it was still true. Why was the truth so shameful to those sows?

Harrison looked out his window at the vast blue tops, people, points, and clock towers, feelings, iron, and brick. He saw brink. He saw clink. He imagined the future with both Claire and Ginette.

Ginette was very social. He could take her anywhere, and she in turn would take him. She liked to schmooze and so did he. She was thin, pretty, dark. A wisp with substance. She would not be a burden, embarrassment, or obstacle to the approval of other people. She was of mixed parentage. Her father was Columbian and her mother was from the District of Columbia. Her father had gone to Columbia and her mother was born on Columbus Day. This made her interesting. She would be an asset. She'd been schooled in Romania, Moravia, Batavia, Bavaria, and L.A. Petite, attractive, slender, sharp, small, and tiny. Like many Third World aristocrats, she'd call him out in public with small intimate rebukes that would humanize him in the minds of others and telegraph *hot tamale*. It would reveal him as sexy and a good sport. She had friends, she could take care of herself. She was sexy like a tree, all sinew and bone. She had a fencing coach and did Thai massage three times a week. She'd never get sick. She'd never cry over something that couldn't get fixed. She wouldn't lose her passion because she wouldn't settle for its diminishment without discarding all interest. When he was busy, she'd find other things to do.

These were all good points.

Claire, on the other hand, was very slow. She'd never send the little note, never make the spontaneous gesture within the right framework of time. She wouldn't introduce him to anything exterior that he couldn't find for himself. Her world was small. She had interior beauty, true. But so do many others. Hers wasn't unique in the fact of its existence, only in its precision. Choosing her would mean a romantic retreat from the world of competition. *La petite vie*. And that would prove what a man he truly was. That he didn't need the glare of the flashbulbs in his own living room. It would be true love. Just choosing Claire. No world included.

He thought about that. Just Claire. No World. Just Claire. No World. Just Claire. No World.

Could be ultimately dull.

If he and Ginette fought there would still be something interesting to do. With Claire, they would have no choice but to read.

That settled it. The choice was clear. Ginette.

And yet the choice of Claire seemed dangerously and repulsively inevitable. He might not have to pull the wool over her eyes. Maybe she would accept him as he truly was. A scoundrel. Was it better to be known or unknown? Ginette was superficial; she would never see what was wrong. Claire would notice right away.

Harrison Bond believed that there was one woman, somewhere on this earth, who could understand him and accept him for the bastard that he truly was. A woman from whom he would never have to hide, his equal. He could trust her and she wouldn't go away, even if he did something wrong. That was the woman he would love forever, the one who would love him forever. Not *accept* with recrimination, tears, and tragic resignation. But simply accept, with pleasure.

Perhaps neither of these gals fit that bill.

9. THEY WERE NICE

I FINISHED MY article with Nadine's loving coach/touch/couch. Her fascination with Glick was bordering on insane fandom. She was doodling the words *ambition* and *flesh and bone* on our dishtowels. She was playing old Ornette Coleman music and anything else that took her back to the avant-gardish days. She even started wearing clothes that had never returned into style, like moccasins and midi-skirts, jumpsuits and sparkle socks. Anything to stand apart.

I combed my hair, clutched my article under my arm, and set out for Mr Bond's.

While I was wandering through the colorful and strangely happy streets, I did not know that Bond was still thinking about the two dames in his life, and still trying to choose. The main problem was that they were both nice. He would have preferred if both of them could be happy. In fact, he knew he could keep both of them happy if they would just grow up enough to let him have everything his way. He could win the approval of both sets of their friends.

But in the meantime, Harrison needed a title for his second novel. *My Sperm* was really hard to beat. There were very few words in the English language that carried that same weight as the word "sperm." Only "Mom."

The problem with "Mom" was that she wasn't provocative. All her meanings were already known. She suffered, and—depending on your school of thought—it was her fault or someone else's. "Sperm" was unique in its power. It still elicited a slight frisson in casual conversation. All you had to do was say it and someone would laugh. It was naturally surprising.

Harrison had realized quite early in the title search that going for another key word was not the best approach. It would clearly be a pale imitation. The new title had to have a lot of different sounds and some overlapping images. It had to appear to be a title so foreign from his first that the content and direction of the second novel would be completely unpredictable. Like *Mongol Siblings in Shreveport*. Something a little gothic. Second novels shouldn't be as easy as the first ones — not on the writer and not on the public. They should telegraph *stretch*, thereby showing the artist's inevitable trajectory to the big, big leagues.

He shuffled papers at his desk, looking for a great idea. Plot clot. A murder, did it have to be a murder? Couldn't child abuse, a nice violent rape, couldn't that suffice? A homosexual killer who rapes his victims through their eye sockets? A woman who viciously murders prostitutes? Something unpredictable. A black jazz musician who takes drugs and the white people who learn from his mistakes? A good story.

A doorbell awoke him from unsettling dreams.

"Hi."

It was me.

He shuddered.

"Hi, Harrison," I smiled insecurely. "Did you forget our appointment?"

"Oh no," he sneered, feigning politeness while clearly letting me know that I am nothing. In case I forgot. By using a tonal sneer while saying the right words, he would never be quoted disadvantageously, and yet the message was crystal clear. They teach you this in private school. They teach you how to be the kind of guy who could never be charged with "but you said ..." because he never said it.

I smiled again, trying to connect. He looked everywhere but here.

"Have you got the eight words?"

"Yes," I said, sitting down on his leather sofa, determined to chat. He hated that. Harrison just could not stand the way that the wrong people would sit down next to him expecting something meaningful. It was a time waster. The pressure to get rid of them was too much. He wanted to look the other way, flip a trap door, and never think about those skanks again. He was a God. He could make scum disappear. Looking at me made him want to drink. It was all my fault.

"What have you been doing today?" I asked, trying to make friends. I imagined our future camaraderie. Gin and tonics on his beach house porch in Venice. Me on the back of his motorcycle.

"Thinking of a title for my second novel."

As soon as the words were out of his mouth, he wondered why he had divulged anything. He regretted advancing the conversation because now I would want to talk about it more. And if I was sitting before him blathering, how could I disappear?

He turned, cracked the new bottle of Bombay, and the rest of his day was shot. All because of me.

"I'm sure you're worried," I said. "I am a copywriter, after all, and I know that packaging is more important than the object itself. But, that's what a career is, an art career or any other." I raised my hand high to illustrate. "Ups and ..." I smashed my hand flat on the table. "... downs." Then I did it again. "Ups ... and ... downs." This time I smashed the table harder. "Downs are inevitable. It's the bounce-back that counts." I guess I was excited.

Harrison hated that word. *Downs*. He despised it and anyone who used it.

"It is not inevitable," he said. "Look at Phillip Roth."

"Maybe you'll be that lucky," I smiled. I thought I was being reassuring, but simultaneously wise and knowing. "Sure, I'll have a drink. Thanks!"

We sat on his couch and stared out through his double skylights, drinking. It was the best couch I had ever been on. Comforting but not so soft it would break your back. You could sleep or read without falling asleep, make love, or chat. It was so deep that I didn't have to hold up my own neck. Outside, shades of perfect evening mist streamed in through the urban filter. Light in front of, on top of, beside, and behind buildings, all converging like a vision at Lourdes. But this was a typical city evening now, in a New York where suddenly everything worked miracles.

Harrison hated me so much that he could have chopped up my body with a fork. I had tried to shame him, obviously, but he was too well bred and drunk for that. I was not, however, so I didn't notice the difference. From now on, he would simply ignore me, have another drink. No matter how long I sat there, he would shut up and suck them down. He knew that someday I would just go away. So he drank.

"Oh well," he said finally, when the bottle was half gone. "We'll have to talk again soon." Over his dead body. "You're on the inside now — *The Brand New York* and all that. No more complaints."

"No," I said, handing over my precious piece. "Here are the words. Z-mail me the cash."

When he had politely seen me to the door, and was safely back behind lock and key, Harrison had another Bombay. He was so annoyed. Why had Ginette and Claire put him in this situation? Couldn't they take care of themselves? Why did they let him have so much control? It was humiliating. Protecting them from him was their job, not his. Everybody was driving him crazy. Harrison kicked back and put his head in his hands.

Here was the thing, he drunkenly realized. He did not look for fulfillment in other people. He needed women for something else far more desperate. He needed them for romance, for sex, to talk on the phone, to see at the end of the day. They were time fillers. He did not need them for a sense of self. Was that so bad? He liked to put his arm around a woman in the movies, walk home, make love, and have coffee in the morning. There was nothing in any of that that required one at a time.

What was he going to write about? All of his favorite topics had already been grabbed: his penis, television, kids in New Jersey who don't do anything. Software. Pollution. Maybe he should call his second novel *Gilligan's Island.* That wry, glib, distanced sense of humor that stands for nothing on its own was a sure bet. He loved that way of being, it had taken him and so many like him so very far. Now, supposedly, that was over. But he had no idea of what could possibly take its place.

10. CLAIRE'S GLEE

CLAIRE, THE REAL One with the bad TV, Claire had something holy to write. She went to one of those new-fangled—what are they called?—stationery stores. The word "staples" now only meant tiny metal things that came in cardboard boxes. This particular shop, named *Marge's Corner Stationery Store*, had just opened up where a Wendy's used to be. A nice woman named Marge read mysteries behind the counter while she sold paper and writing instruments. There Claire found some gorgeous paper, rough-hewn. And she also found a neat pen.

Claire sat down in a tea shop and tried to compose, but her arm didn't wrap properly around this brand-new writing utensil. She drank down the Darjeeling, wandered outside, and landed on a stoop, laying out a sheet of gorgeous pulp flat against a book. The book was a gift from Harrison Bond. *Great Short Stories of Honoré de Balzac*.

Although romantic, this pose was hard—sitting on steps, slouching over a pad. Her back would not remain straight enough, straight enough to write. Even after so many hours of yoga. Pens were not so easy to maneuver anymore; most people took classes to learn how to use them. The gorgeous succulent handwriting that she'd imagined came out crude, ugly, and vague. Finally, she gave up, scooted home, checked her mailbox, leaned back in her chair. It was perfect for watching *I Love Lucy*, but not very helpful when it came to using a pen. Its ball did not slide. She felt every bump and grind of the paper's weave. It was like riding your bike over backwoods underbrush. Then she tried the kitchen table, perfect for wine or oatmeal. But for writing the truest letter from her heart, it was too slick. The paper slid. Finally, Claire just stopped posing and did it. She scrawled with passion across the top of the page, knowing that the formation of her letters and their links would never be beautiful. She felt like Queen Victoria with dyslexia. Her handwriting sucked. It expressed, but did not communicate.

Finally, Claire accepted her limitations, and turned on the computer with a clap of her hands. There she composed a missive to her secret true love. And his name was NOT Harrison Bond.

Dear Jeff,

Every day at the appointed times, I go to the mailbox and await each Postal Round to see if there is a letter for me from you.

I know that Sophinisba reinstated letter writing as a way to create jobs and reverse the speedup process provoked by email, and most importantly so that we can all have better interpersonal relationships.

I think she has a good idea there, I really do. Gee whiz, I sound like a bimbo. A really authoritative person would say, "SHE HAS A GOOD IDEA." Not "I THINK." I'm not the female Sambo, brains akimbo. It's just that twenty-four hours a day of mail service and delivery, more employment, more incentive, cheaper stamps—all that seems cool. But it also means that I have five opportunities per twenty-four hours to be disappointed by your silence.

Jeff, darling, I remember when phone-answering machines were first invented. I didn't want to leave home because I had no way of knowing whether or not a message was waiting. I hoped that my father would call to apologize, and I didn't want to miss it.

Then they invented access codes and I could beep in every fifteen minutes, all day long. Whenever I felt anxiety about my father's good-guy type of cruelty, I would call my machine and hope. It was expensive, all those quarters, but cheaper than hospitalization.

Then they invented cell phones. I didn't have to carry bags of quarters with me and spend time stopping at pay phones, looking for one that wasn't broken. Now every time I felt anxious and missed my father's ever absent love, I could make the phone call to my machine, but still keep walking.

Everything was faster, faster, faster. Even though he never called. Then I met you.

But now, with all of these mail deliveries, I've had to change my life again. I can't leave the house to go to work at The MEDIA HUB without enormous fear that your letter is waiting for me back home in the box.

Even though my father is now dead, I hope that in his final moments he realized that he had hurt me and wrote a letter of apology that has since gotten lost in the mail. And that, in the end, he actually did love me more than his own ego, right? So now I spend weekends waiting for the sound of the Post-Teen punching in the combination on the front door.

The way I look at it, Jeff my love, EITHER:

1. You want to write things to me that are difficult to convey, but you can't put yourself through that and nothing else worth sending comes to mind.

OR

2. You don't know what to say.

Jeff, I project onto you all day long. How ironic, since my job is to design ROM-Projectiles for Five Dimensional Nasal Imaging. My emotions and my day job have become low- and high-tech versions of the same process.

Jeffrey, dear Jeffrey, I am fast and you are slow. I want answers as soon as I've gleaned the question, and when nothing is gleaned, I want questions to answer. I want proof of my impact on you. I want to save you. I want you to save me. I want to rescue you. I want you to rescue me. I want us to transform each other, thereby healing each other. And I want it now. I can't wait to save my own life by saving yours, and you saving your life the same way.

You are vague and confused, Jeff-O. You give vague, confused answers. On the surface, you appear to be brain dead or, at least, a moron. You like something, but you can't explain why and you won't bother to think about it. You take antidepressants so you can't have any orgasms, but you're always hard. This makes you more depressed, but less depressed than you would be without the antidepressants. If you don't take your meds, you won't even kiss.

For you, Jeffie, just saying that you like something is a big confession. Get over it. You are not so special that you can be ashamed of things that everyone else does too. CONNECT. CONNECT. Take a look around, you dope. Everyone else is scared too, and that's what it is to be human. Only a narcissist thinks he is the only one who is scared. And that he has to withhold, or else has to recognize himself in others. You're racked with guilt and blame yourself for everything to the point of negative megalomania.

Well, blame me, darling! Blame me!

Let me at least give you that much.

Confession for me is de rigueur. I don't pretend to be so special. In fact, I am so regular, like everyone else, that I recognize myself in others compulsively. I see everyone else's faults as forgivable, and so I forgive myself. Maybe I need more shame. And that is something you

can give me. With your eyes closed. It would be so easy for you, Jeff.
You would be excellent at it. That's what you offer me, the shame that
I so desperately need. Please do it.

   Love,

   Claire

11. FORMER RUSSIANS

ON THE WAY home from Harrison's, I stopped off to do the dinner grocery shopping at the former Organic Wal-Mart. Now it was a free-for-all, with people selling tomatoes out of their window boxes, and home-made refrigerator cake. There, I spotted one.

You see, I have had a lifelong hobby of recognizing former Soviet Bloc celebrities in the supermarket. This interest began in childhood. My father used to like to stop prominent individuals on the street and have them shake my hand, so that later (like now) I could say that that was what we did. In this manner I met James Baldwin when I was six. I met Dave Madden from *Laugh-In*. And then, one day, in the Daitch-Shopwell, by the dairy case …

"Look," Daddy said. "That's Alexander Kerenski."

"Who's that?"

"The Prime Minister of the Menshevik government of Russia, after the Czar and before the Communists."

I looked up from behind his knee. The object of my father's fandom was a lonely old man in an old gray suit. He was food shopping slowly because it was his only way to be around people. His suit was too big on him because he was well into the shrinking process. Poor guy, he placed his bets on the wrong side of history and paid ever since. Nowadays, Mr Kerenski would ask people questions like, "What kind of sour cream do you like?" just to hear another human voice interact with his own. He dreamed that one of these people would strike up a conversation and become his friend. That they could have tea together and talk about the Duma, the Cossacks, and Lenin, that scoundrel. But this never happened. He saw it take place once in a movie and twice in a play, but in real life one thing never led to another. Kerenski stopped. He changed his glasses, stalling for more time among the living. He examined the sour cream container again. What was he looking for? The refrigeration refreshed his soul. He changed his mind, reached for the cottage cheese.

"Look," my father said, young and robust, large key ring dangling by his side. He had always wanted to be great, the world's best Super. But he did not hold his thwarted wish against others who truly were great, nor those who had failed but tried. This generosity came, in part, from the fact that no one on earth was considered the World's Best Superintendent. He aspired to a goal that no one else could attain either.

"He used to be the ruler of Russia."

I stared, transfixed. This is what happens to kings, stars, the most powerful of men. They can be reduced to standing next to me. "Look," my father whispered. "Look at him now. He can't even chew."

What a lesson. So many years later, I carry this warning from my dear old dad. Nothing matters except Nadine.

As an adult, I avoided mass-produced edible treats, and only bought organics that were tasty and overpriced. Now, though, at People's Market, there was unlimited choice. Not just fifty-seven kinds of cheese, but 157. And each was named after its maker: Steve Cheese, Joanne Cheese, Ludwig Cheese, Jr.

And standing there, in front of the acres of personal cheese, I had my own adult paternal memorial Slavic celebrity sighting. Anna Kornslyovichkowaskyski. In her day, she had been the darling of the Party. The grandsons of the overthrowers of Kerenski had made her a star. She could have tea in her coffee while the People just got educated. Now, though, with the former Soviet Union in subdivisions that would make Long Island jealous, she lived in New York buying potatoes right out of the earth. Here at People's Market, you dig them yourself.

"Hi," I said. "If I had a child of my own, I would have him shake your hand."

"You know me?" She smiled.

"Yes," I said, reaching for the shake. "You were the most privileged and corrupt movie star in all of the CCCP."

"Yes," she said, smiling for the cameras. "That will always be true. Even when I am dead. Film curators with fetishes for kitsch will dig up my films and feel some pang of desire. No matter what they know intellectually, they will never lose that little *ooooohhhh* one feels in the presence of a star."

"What do you do now?" I asked.

"I work in THE MEDIA HUB." She looked tragic. It was lovely. She had found resilience, and then triumph of the human spirit.

"Thank you," I said. "Your performance reminds me of what really matters in life. It is healing and transformative."

I was thinking about Nadine, and a smile came to my tongue.

"You're welcome," she answered, burdened by the history of Mother Russia and ten pounds of laundry detergent. "The mighty must fall, and yet, they once were mighty." And then she wheeled down the aisle towards the condiments.

I stopped, surrounded by red kale, purple sage, lemon chard, radish greens. All of these should make up Nadine's bed. Let her lie on a throw of sweet, clean, leafy vegetables. A blanket of nutrients. I admired her. And secretly, in that store, I worshipped her.

Treat your lover like Lord Krishna, unless she thinks she's Lord Krishna.

I shopped with love. I carried my groceries home with purpose. I cooked them with delight and served them with desire. Every mundane action was carried out with love. I realized that I had the human anchor. I did not need the glory of Harrison Bond, and I did not need the price of kowtowing to his cowlick. I had something better. Something real. I had Nadine to love. And so I resolved to stay at my boring job, stay at my maintenance income, stay at my level of achievement, and swell in my love for Nadine. Who I knew was not thinking of me at all, because she too is real, and serves her own purpose.

I went outside and stood, staring up at my gorgeous new city. Thank you Sophinisba, for letting me in just enough to see that I don't need the glitz. Wow, she was a genius. Taking the obstacles down gave us more free choice in our lives. Removing the poison of glamor made my life singularly better. Who needed Bond? Not I.

And in the moment I was filled with my love for Nadine, her enormous wish, the pleasure of my life. I was filled with joy.

12. A WORKING GIRL FROM THE WORKING CLASS

OF THE TWO women who Harrison loved, only one—Claire Sanchez—was a working girl from the Bronx.

Like other blue-collar women in the age of empty and compulsive overqualification, she had a Master's Degree in Techno-Scription and one in Visual Cues. All day long she designed pages for Ad-Month, Ad-Week, Ad-Day, and Ad-Minute.

Everyday she designed cyberpages that were not real pages for stores that were not real stores. And they all belonged to each other, merged and managed by sinister mysterious and imprecise forces. There was no material plane.

But Claire increasingly noticed, with some surprise, when she walked down the street, that under the new regime every store was different. Yet when she went to work, all the cyberpages remained the same.

This was very odd.

Since THE CHANGE, two entirely different cultures seemed to be co-inciting. One was outside, on the street—where each store, sign, design, outfit, motif, and moment were different. The other was inside, online—where it all remained the same.

When walking lazily on a Sunday afternoon, on the way to and from Competitive Yoga class, Claire could pop in and out of all kinds of eccentric experiences, make singular purchases. The birds chirped, the wind blew, the rain scattered, and everything around her was individual.

But as soon as she stepped inside her apartment or office and turned on the computer, it was all mass-produced and homogenized. On the pink and blue sidewalks, next to those logo-free buildings, she would never think about buying a brand name. But when she turned on the machine, her mind changed. Suddenly Consistency and Familiarity were the most comforting of all.

This was the compromise that Sophinisba had struck between Business and Humanity.

Walking down streets that all had the same stores had proven to be depressing. More and more New Yorkers were complaining of repetition compulsion. The reason that they lived in NYC was to see something new every block. Without that, they felt trapped. With branches of the same bank next to the same fast-food coffee shop on Seventh Street, Eighth Street, Ninth Street, and Tenth, people were getting sadder, and could no longer have crazy, wild great ideas and then carry them out. They already felt defeated by the time they got to work in the morning. The city had become boring. Which made them deranged.

Before THE CHANGE, New Yorkers were becoming increasingly confused. They could not remember where they were. Differentiation therapists were thriving, but everyone else was schizophrenic. With the removal of all that sameness, the only conformity was through computer screens and mail. Even alienation had become depersonalized.

Claire had seen that bad stuff unfold and knew that things were a lot more hopeful now. And yet, she felt an uneasy sense of balance. There was a different city outside her door than behind it. Her computers were all inside, although they claimed to be access to the out. Yet nothing outside resembled the world found on her screens, the world within. Claire noticed this regularly and it made her itch.

She was feeling similarly about Harrison—itchy. And getting

nowhere with Jeff.

I go through men like telephone poles, she thought.

This thought was some kind of slogan. An ad for her own consciousness. But what did it mean besides a penile allusion? Most ads had sexual innuendo but no meaning, and now her feelings did too. Did people go through telephone poles? It was the other way around, like Frida Kahlo. Or did she mean telephone *polls*, where they ask you a question to try to make you buy? Even devoid of meaning, the phrase sounded reasonable. It sounded provocative, sexual, dangerous, wise, and glib. It sounded ironic and know-it-all, but it actually meant nothing. It was a facsimile of an idea. *This is what happens*, Claire noted with objective horror, *to people who live advertising, i.e., all people.* They had thoughts that sounded meaningful, but weren't. Minds were changing, getting smaller. Including hers.

Maybe it was all subconsciously because of Harrison's title about his sperm, or maybe his sperm was just another reflection of the pre-existing trend. Excitement about using references to men's genitals had overtaken the country. Everyone metaphored someone else's cock. It was like saying "okay" or "whatever." A habit.

Claire's ex-best friend, Ginette, whom she now demonized, had once told her:

"You need to be fucked by a tree."

This could be interpreted as prophetic, since they were now both taking turns sitting on the engorged penis of the same very tall Harrison Bond. But also, Ginette had not intended that statement as an erotic prediction, but rather meant to imply she thought that Claire was a major cunt. It was a put-down. Something about a woman's vagina being large around meant something demeaning about her character and soul.

Now, remembering that bitch Ginette, Claire had a new take on the meaning of her thought, *I go through men like telephone poles.*

She and Ginette had once driven down a country road decorated by former trees that were now working for the phone company. This was when they were friends and were on their way to have Christmas with Ginette's parents in an exotic part of West Virginia. They kept passing the poles, passing the poles, which all looked just the same. That's what Claire felt about men. They were wildly different individuals, but her feelings of doom were interchangeable. While memories of Ginette remained uniquely painful.

Whew! Relief!

She had realized something about herself that wasn't about a product.

There was still some content to her interior life. Where would that lead? She had to choose between Harrison, who was himself choosing, and Jeff, who ignored her completely.

How to decide?

Harrison Bond was a big old brute. Of that, Claire was sure. He always hinted at a desire to fuck her in the ass, not softly and carefully, as they had done a couple of times already. But rather, with a lot more force. He wanted to tear her insides to shreds.

"I want to tear your insides to shreds," he'd panted.

Fortunately, his penis was just too big for that much action, so she had plenty of reason to deflect his rectal rage.

He cried a lot, that Harrison. He was so sad. Sometimes when Claire was dreaming about her true love, Jeff, she would happen to have a psychic glance at Harrison and see his despair. His big secret was that he could not feel cool about himself, and he told her so. Many times. It was fun, that kind of intimacy. They both loved every second of it. The had each, in the past, yearned for this and thrown it away. Now they both had the same chance for redemption. Claire would rub Harrison's belly and he would confess his self-loathing. Trying, trying to reach out and connect. He did not know that she secretly loved Jeff. He'd never heard of Jeff. He thought that this distance between him and Claire was natural, and it made him feel safe. He had no idea that she was really dreaming of another man.

In these moments Harrison assessed, mistakenly, that he could probably find another woman any time he wanted to, but that if Claire ever got sick of his weird ways, she would probably be alone.

Sometimes Claire was so upset about Jeff that she tore out her eyebrows. The last time she did this they did not grow back, and she had to get permanent makeup tattooed over her eyes. Harrison never noticed.

Jeff is a kook, true, she thought lovingly. *But maybe, just maybe, he will help me learn something about myself that would equal the kind of peace I felt when he'd rubbed my back.*

Every single boyfriend she'd ever had, had come to a time when he no longer wanted to rub her back. He was too tired. It was the sign. Of doom.

Claire had a terrible fear of uselessness, that all the labors of her life would come to nothing. All that loving, come to nothing. There was a great ambiguity at the center of Claire's existence that had followed her all of her days.

Help! Help!

"Fate!" she cried, waiting for the mail. "Please make all my decisions for me."

13. FATHERHOOD

AND WHO WAS this guy, Jeff? The Withholder, with so many fates in his unwilling hands? Jeff lived on the Fourthside of town and had two sons: Dominick and Freddy.

Dominick was in rehab. Freddy was in detox. That's the kind of father Jeff was.

Frankly, Jeff had never done a thing to help his kids. Every sentence he'd ever muttered to either of them had started with the word YOU and was then followed by a delineation of how bad they were, or how wrong.

"You, nobody wants you here."

"You, you're wrong, kid. You're a wrong kid."

That sort of thing.

Of course, there were reasons for this. As Sigmund Freud noted, families have cultures like countries, and patterns of pain are reproduced from generation to generation. Obviously, Jeff's own father had also been inadequate, and it was a good bet that that guy's dad was in the same boat. Etcetera.

Nonetheless, we live in the moment, and the handing down of pain defines Jeff's fatherhood.

The way that Mayor Sophinisba Breckinridge's policies affected Jeff's damaged life was that, in the past, he would have been financially responsible for trying to fix the kids. Since he was inept, he never would have had the money, and Dominick and Freddy would have been detritus in the sea of life. But now, with the new Mediserve System, Jeff was not the only person who had to cough up the cash for the consequences of his earlier inactions. Others would chip in. So Dominick and Freddy actually got the treatment they needed and, therefore (under the new system), deserved. Simply by having been born.

That's why Jeff was such a wreck at the time Claire fell in love with him. Not only was he his old bad self, but he also suffered from lack of penance in the face of all the pain he had caused.

Ah, the unforeseen nature of forgiveness without amends, it gives the transgressor nothing to wish for.

Fuck that bitch, Sophinisba, Jeff thought. *She took all my responsibilities away. Now I have nothing to shirk or pretend.*

It was a horrible burden, this loss. He felt excluded from a dynamic relationship to the world. Remember, treating someone awfully is still a relationship, no matter how paltry. For some people, inflicting undeserved pain is the only intimacy they are capable of. Take away their ability to hurt someone they should love, and then what?

Jeff lay on his dirty, embarrassing couch with Claire, all curled up in their post-shower towel. There was a drop of water on her exquisite shoulder. That is what life is all about at its best.

Stay here, he begged internally. *Stay here. Stay in this ecstatic moment. Wait, don't move. Why do they have to move?*

She ran her fingers through his long, balding, boring hair before departing. He knew where she was going. To Harrison's house.

Jeff saw himself being loved. It was cinematic, unreal. The woman departing, leaving her fingertips in his hair. It wasn't a real feeling. It was someone else's image. He felt love. He felt dead.

Since she loved him, why was she leaving? Because that's what people do. They like to destroy. Jeff looked at her blankly, but inside he was a wreck. Claire thought she was benign, but she was genocidal. How could someone miss a detail like that about themselves?

What Jeff could not imagine was that his thin banal hair reminded Claire of her beloved late grandfather's hair. And that, therefore, his head held meaning for her that did not originate with him.

Claire's grandfather gave her unconditional love and a back rub every night. Jeff could have no idea of all the associations working in his favor. He thought all that love was for him alone. He squeaked out the words

I love you.

Jeff had not uttered that phrase in fifteen years—hence, two addicts for sons. Long ago, there had been another human walking the earth to whom he could honestly say "I love you," but she was too much of an asshole to let him say it. She hung up the phone every time he called. FOR FIFTEEN YEARS. That's how fearful she was of the truth. A Life Waster.

This time, with Claire, it came out of his mouth like blood.

It was devastating. It was something.

Being that close to tenderness and not being able to possess it. All because of that fucking Harrison Bond. His rival.

14. GIN

As YOU CAN see, the lure of potential power had changed my mind completely. The entire focus of my consciousness had become the jet-ski set. The glams: Harrison, Claire, Ginette. They were all suddenly more important to me than I was.

Nadine noticed this occasionally, as she was busy focusing all her mental attention on Glick and the promise of being a pure artist.

Each of us was seduced by our fantasies of people who did not know us or think about us. Nadine and I were consumed by one-way spiritual relationships with imagined personalities who didn't give a shit about either of us. We had marketed ourselves right out of our intimacy.

And that was somehow so comforting.

It was like being on TV instead of in front of it.

We pretended and pretended that other lives were our lives, and the days went by.

Meanwhile, back in Bombay, Harrison was still mad. Ginette was coming over to his pad in an hour and he still had not started his amazing second novel. Too much was at stake. Looking for inspiration, he picked up a jar of hand lotion and read the label:

1.7 fl oz

Hey, that might make a good title!

Or, how about a groovier version?

One Point Seven Flozz.

Now there is a prize-winning book.

He could coin a phrase, *flozz,* uh, a word.

Harrison picked up some copy for the next week's issue of BNY. That stupid bitch (me!) had given him eight pages instead of eight words. What a moron. He knew it was a set-up. He'd cut it down to eight words himself, and then she'd yell *prejudice.*

Exhausted, he just took the first eight words. They were fine enough. No one would read them anyway; it was just a bone to The New Era.

Tired, he keyed them into the graphascope.

Passion interrupts me on the hot sun porch.

That would be a great title for his novel. It was so sensitive. It conveyed everything that he wanted to convey about himself. They'd call it *Passion* for short. But it wouldn't have the risky weight of actually being named *Passion.* That would just be its nickname. Like *Gatsby.* Everyone forgets about *The Great* that preceded it.

What a fantastic manipulation of both reader and bookseller.

Coerced, Harrison began to type:

Passion Interrupts Me on a Hot Sun Porch
by Harrison Bond

CHAPTER ONE

I am not my sperm.

The doorbell rang. It was Ginette, just in time to ruin his concentration.

But, *hey,* he felt, reaching for the bottle.

Ginette was the unique person in his life. She'd

marked him. She'd promised him a permanence he didn't need—then. The second he'd come around to the idea, she would pull out the rug. But because they were so wonderful as a public couple, no one would believe his version, and he'd be ruined, eternally.

Ha. Ha. Ha.

She'd change him into a mealy, needy, clingy man.

Then, only he would know that she was very, very mean. Everyone else would only notice her good manners and nice shoes.

This, consequently, would put Harrison on the defensive. He would have to be extra-specially nice and accommodating and do whatever she said just to keep her from hurting his feelings. Even the thought was exhausting. It dried him up. It made him unable to leave the relationship because he would never recover. Furthermore, it was tragic.

Everything else about her was right.

He waited. He was waiting, hoping every single morning that she would change her nasty ways. That she would no longer snap at him for wanting to look at the blurbs on the backs of book jackets and for being tired. Major crimes like that. If Ginette could just check it, they could both live happily ever after and polish each other's mirrors. Why didn't she want them to be happy together? He had no idea.

15. TWO

As for me, your Emcee?

When two people love each other, they sometimes forget to mention it. In those natural trancelike dry spells, strange transformations take place in the dark. For example, they could each find entirely new interior lives and change their relationship in a snap. Like that.

Nadine had fallen obsessively in love with a woman in her office, but she never mentioned it to me. Between Glick and Love Object Girl, letting me in on it slipped her mind. Many times she called this woman and then hung up the phone. Called her, and then hung up the phone.

Amazingly, this woman's name was ... Ginette.

Can you imagine? For weeks, my Nadine had only two thoughts: *Glick, Ginette. Glick, Ginette.* But she only said "Glick" in my presence.

Whenever I found her daydreaming, I would ask:

"Honey? What's up with you?"

And she would recover by lying.

"Oh," she'd hum, "I was just wishing that I could paint non-marketable images like Glick instead of sitting at a computer doing graphic design."

Okay, so the first time I heard this, I thought it was true. A truthful wish. And I was moved by her tender smile.

But the next time it happened, something started to sink in, it was that sinking-in feeling. My lover's dissatisfaction was before me like her cunt on a plate. Her frustration twitched. I suddenly grokked that she was walking around all day dreaming of a better, different life. I didn't want her to go there alone. So I woke up, got off my own horse, and focused everything on what we both wanted for her,

I thought about her more and more. How could I help Nadine realize her dream? What could I do? We were in this life together, after all. And I began to look differently at my own day. I tried to picture a way to better our common situation, RIGHT NOW.

Yet this new desire, designed by both of us to bring us closer together, was all a ruse. A ruse named … Ginette.

I think that if Nadine had actually spoken to Ginette, if she had had a full conversation, perhaps it all would have ended differently. But she was afraid, and so Nadine withheld her true feelings from both Ginette and I. The more she withheld, the more repression Nadine engendered, the stronger and stranger the tension between Nadine and her world. After many, many weeks of lying, Nadine decided to see if she and Ginette could become friends.

She started saying "hi" in the hallways of THE MEDIA HUB.

Ginette looked the other way.

She sat next to her at lunch.

Ginette spent the whole meal programming her cell phone to turn on her air conditioning back home.

The more Nadine tried to create a situation of mutual human acknowledgement, the more Ginette withheld. The more she withheld, the stronger the tension.

After all, withholding doesn't wither. Its force is cumulative. This is what my hero Walter Benjamin called AURA. The false power of distance.

I hate withholders. Especially the seductive kind. They cause ruin.

One day, Nadine and I were walking down the street and we passed Ginette. Nadine smiled weakly and Ginette smiled falsely.

"Hi," Ginette said vaguely, and then kept walking.

I didn't realize that this was the first time Ginette had ever actually spoken to Nadine. I didn't even know that Ginette existed. All I saw was some kind of superficial smirk on the face of a strange but chic woman. I knew, subconsciously, that Nadine was being snubbed.

As a result of this experience, I too started thinking about Ginette.

Thinking of myself as more curious than Nadine would ever be, I started secretly searching for information about Ginette. Who was this charismatic withholder? I found out a lot of stuff that didn't matter, but it added dimension.

Then, one night, I was listening to a conversation outside my window. It was the iceman, come to repair the elevator. He said,

"I guess you identified with her."

As soon as I heard the word "identified," I did it. It was like hypnosis. Later, I found out that the iceman was a hypnotist, working on elevators on the side. I identified with Nadine's unspoken obsession with Ginette. That's how tuned in we were.

That night I dreamed that I had called Ginette and hung up the phone. I woke up, filled with regret. *Why did I do that?* I wondered. I thought, somehow, that I had become inexplicable and ruined my own life.

It took most of the morning to assimilate that this had only been a dream. That, in fact, I was not calling up strange people who owed me nothing and asking for something. Acknowledgement. That's what those kind of phone calls are about, are they not?

And so on.

Nadine became more and more distant. Because I had compassion for Nadine, and could accept her consciously and subconsciously for who she is, I admired her. What I admired most about her was that she was a woman who could be distant, but still elicit the kind of love from me that I wished to feel from her. I hoped that someday, soon, Nadine would wake up again, remember that she also accepted and admired me, and we could get back to the equilibrium we had worked so hard to reach.

Given the sudden lack of mutual attention, I realized that Nadine was doing something right and I was doing something wrong because she had all of my love, but I only had part of hers.

She had me listening, empathizing, forgiving.

I had her barely noticing.

Therefore she was more worthy and someone to be adored.

In this new state, I admired her more and more each day. I longed to be more and more like her, in order to be loved the way she was. I longed to be seen—and not at a waning lover's mercy.

Clearly, for the first time since this story began, I was in pain.

Why?

Strangely, I decided it was a Bond thing. My themes had converged. Although it had been clear to me for some time that Harrison Bond was never going to get back to me, I found that hard to accept. I mean, if I needed to blow someone off, I'd call them and let them know. But to pretend that there was a "Big Change," and then leave me hanging in the old style—that sucked.

But Nadine's turning away woke up his abandonment big time. It was twosies. Twice removed. Which made the Bond thing hurt more.

Basically, I had been diminished by Harrison pulling that old-style switcheroo. That's when they tell you to call them, and then you do, and they never call you back, and you keep calling, and then you become a pest, and then they say bad things about you to other people, about what a pest you are—while never, ever mentioning or remembering that they told you to call in the first place. At this point, calling becomes a futile act with no one ever at the other end. While all along you thought it was right to keep your word and follow through, but there ain't another soul who seems to agree.

Bewildered as to why I was being excluded simply for following directions, I became emotionally disheveled. Bedeviled. Satanic. In fact, I became the flea in the elephant's nose. All I could do to make myself feel better was to think about Ginette every day and night. It was the only action I could take where I knew for sure that I wasn't the only one doing it.

I asked Nadine about my conundrum, but since her love was diminished, she decided that I had superceded my quota of how many times I could discuss the problem of others not calling back. She said it was a fact of life, like the stars, and that that was that.

"What do you suggest instead?" I asked, admiring her so.

"Hold the pain inside you," she whispered, turning out all the lights. "Then, accumulate that dark, dark sadness that all repressed irresolution accumulates. Become a darkly sad person with too much to explain to anyone new, and therefore do not accrue or maintain friends."

"Okay," I said. Such was my lot, apparently, thanks to Bond Fucker.

Feeling apocalyptic, I took a story and threw it out the window. It was called "Two," and it was written by Isaac Bashevis Singer.

90

16. TOO

IRONICALLY, AND YET naturally—since we are often connected to each other by chance, wish, design, task, fate, aesthetics, fear, antiques, stamp-collecting, faux cheese for vegans, technology, horses, Turkmenistan, and gout—Jeff's son Freddy had gotten a release job working garbage detail, and it was through this path that he got hold of that same discarded story.

In the Yiddish world, Isaac Bashevis Singer was not called Singer. He was called Bashevis. Had it been up to the Yiddish readers to select their own choice for the Nobel Prize, they would have preferred his brother, I.J. Singer. In Yiddish, when you say *Singer*, you mean the brother. Odd, isn't it? How defenseless minor languages must tolerate the selection of their representative heroes by the Swedish Academy. I.J. wrote long, epic Russian-style novels in Yiddish about such serious topics as the industrialization of Lodz. They were filled with characters: gamblers, prostitutes, laborers, bosses, the religious, the antireligious, and the dark soot streaming out of the factories' chimneys. Some Yiddishists believed that Bashevis got the Nobel Prize because he wrote about sex, something the *goyim* seem to love.

Freddy, knowing none of this, adored the story "Two." He read it over and over again, carrying its tattered pages in the front pocket of his no-label pants. It was the kind of dream that only a found story, floating through the air over a pile of garbage, can bring to a man just out of the Tank. Its entrance into his New Life gestured toward some possibility of justice buried deeply within fate.

In this story, two boys studied together on the same bench,

sharing one volume. It was a romance.

Together they came across an Ecclesiastical phrase. The rough cloth of their trousers serenaded each other's thighs as they contemplated meaning on a smooth wooden slab. In this manner, they learned sensual experience and intellectual perplexity at the same moment. They fell in love, and therefore had to flee to a faraway land. Nothing bad had happened to them yet, but they knew that it would. They had to flee their true homes and then misrepresent themselves in their new home to avoid an inevitable degradation.

Later, the very people who had originated the threat claimed they had never done anything to hurt these boys. And, somehow, sneakily, that was true. They were brilliant, these people. They managed to enforce a thorough condition of deviance on the lads. One so complete that it required their anonymity, exile, and humiliation. And yet, the perpetrators never had to carry out any of the understood threat. In other words, their hands were clean while the job got done.

The race is not to the swift.

That was the biblical phrase that bonded these lovers. They discovered it together, at the same time, holding one book on two laps.

Other, more protected classmates interpreted those words to mean that a goal can be attained equally through slow steady preparation and caution as it can through speed. They thought this in the standard way that protected people miss all subtlety.

The boys, however, knew otherwise. They agreed, soft heads together over a crumbling book, that the phrase had a far more sinister meaning.

You see, they had been punished, but they had not done anything wrong.

As a result, they knew for a fact that there was no justice.

This gave them knowledge that the unpunished did not possess.

They knew that the most qualified is not necessarily the most recognized. And that if he is the most recognized, it may not be because of his qualification. It may be because of who he knows, his skills being of secondary consideration. He may just be the right caste. A born winner. Even if he's not really good enough.

In other words, the fastest may not win the race, even though he is the fastest. The less skilled may reap the reward. And their winning may mean nothing about merit.

A-ha!

The boys took this phrase as a confirmation of a profound, unmovable corruption at the center of social life. That was why they knew to flee.

When they settled in their new faraway home, one passed as a woman. This was to avoid more punishment. When she accidentally died, thirty years later, by slipping on a wet tile and cracking her skull against the floor of the mikva, the villagers realized that she was a man. And being villagers, they sought out his lover and murdered him. The villagers thought this was appropriate. Then both bodies were thrown outside of the cemetery walls to rot.

17. LONGEVITY

FREDDY PUT DOWN this story. Sadly, he had to return to the reality of life outside those pages. But something inside him had been stirred.

Unlike the boys, Freddy was not a homosexual. But he longed for unity with another man, his brother. He wished they could run away together and share everything.

And he saw the arrival of "Two" into his life as a positive omen, because this was the very day that he and his brother Dominick were graduating from the halfway house.

The truth of the matter was that Dominick was the real junkie. He was the one who had the brain chemistry requiring more and more dope. Freddy just wanted to be with him, so he went along with it. Freddy took the minimal amount of narcotics necessary to keep the two of them together. But, actually, he didn't need drugs one way or the other. He just needed a brother.

This is why the story "Two" affected Freddy so deeply. Once someone has been kicked out of society, they are forced into a situation that may not be safe. That consequence was part of the punishment.

The boys in Singer's story had been together for thirty years. Isn't that much too long for any romantic relationship to remain healthy? What if it is with your own brother? That's for life, right? Freddy was pretty sure that if the two boys in the story got sick of each other, there would be no way out. The shitty other people had trapped them inside a mutual box.

Oh God, there he goes in that dress again, one of them probably thought about the other. But still they could not separate. Why exactly? It would involve some kind of pretending about all they had suffered. That it didn't bond them when it did.

People were allowed to feel things in books that they could never feel in real life. If you even tried in real life to approximate the feelings found in a book, someone would object. But actual people wrote those books, right? Where were they? Freddy didn't know. He just wanted some understanding.

For example, in a book, two people are having an argument. One says,

"I'm leaving!" and heads for the door.

The other says, "Wait!"

The first stops and waits. He hears what the other is saying and realizes that they belong together after all.

In real life, whenever he was in this situation, Freddy would yell "Wait!"

But the person would leave anyway. They never stayed to hear the life-changing news.

I want to live in a book, he cried. And buried his worried face in his dirty hands.

This was one of those self-esteem issues that his counselor, Ginette, kept bringing up. All of Freddy's life he had been told that he was bad and wrong. That he was strange. So when he claimed to be a junkie in order to be near his brother, everyone believed him immediately. No one checked to see if it was actually true. They were relieved he had finally failed so they could stop waiting for it to happen. What had his father, Jeff, threatened him with, night and day, all of his life?

You, you're gonna be alone.

And then Jeff would abandon Freddy to make his threat come true.

If Jeff had been kind instead, Freddy would not be alone. He would have had a father. But the old man wouldn't shut up, thereby making happiness impossible.

If you don't do what I tell you to do, you will be alone. Jeff repeatedly promised.

And yet, when Freddy did try to obey his dad, he discovered that his father's wishes were based on a vague fantasy of who Freddy was and what his life was like. A fantasy that was all about his father being right, and not at all possible for Freddy to fulfill. It was a trap. Dad needed Freddy to be wrong. And so, being a loving son and brother, he was.

You will be alone.

Brothers are for life. Therefore, Freddy had to be with his brother, just to prove his father had made a mistake. Same for those two guys in the book. They had to be together in defiance. Is that any way to live?

Freddy's hair was bright and orange and overgrown. His eyes, deeply green. His jaw was so slack that saliva should have poured forth, but he sucked on his own tongue all day long to avoid those problems. He was fidgety and it embarrassed him. He knew that he could never have a love relationship with a boy or girl because he was so fidgety, he couldn't sleep. He'd hang around whenever he wanted to have sex, and when he was through he would leave. Everyone uniformly hated that about him. It was just not acceptable. Even one special girl would rather that he stayed up all night, keeping her awake talking about whatever was on his mind and fucking. But he would not.

She tried to make him love her in the day and he refused. He said that it would deplete him of his essential energies. She thought he was just too shy to make love in the day and that he could not believe how beautiful she thought he was.

This was her fantasy.

The real deal was that he just did not want to walk around in a haze of lust, all dreamily dysfunctional and strange. He didn't want to feel contented. It was too painful. Then he'd want to commit to her and live with her, sit on a chair with his arms around her, see how beautiful her breasts were, visualize her cunt, sit in two chairs next to each other and read while listening to music. He couldn't stand the pain of imagining that, because when it disappeared, he'd know he was the failure his father had always threatened he would be. His father would be right because he, Freddy, would be alone.

18. HAIR

As COLORFUL AND deeply characterized as Freddy was, his brother Dominick had a very different demeanor. He was plucked. His hair and beard never existed—he had only three eyelashes.

Dominick had pale blue eyes, which provided the only protection for his otherwise defenseless face. He smoked incessantly. His legs had no hair. The only shaggy place on his body was around his genitals, and even there it was five thin strands of silver.

Orange-haired Freddy, on the other hand, was outwardly tormented. His face was wrong. Wrong kinds of expressions popped up at all moments. He chewed his jaw, which set all his facial muscles in discomforting directions. Dominick was quiet, different. He barely spoke. His body was flaccid. He would stand still and quiet, bringing the cigarette to and from his lips. The boys were aware that the entire society had changed while they were in treatment, and that the Outside had become a world of more possibility than either of them had ever known. They each feared the opportunity for opportunity. They were shaky.

That is how each of these guys greeted his new life in the New World.

Freddy and Dominick stood outside the gate, the halfway house behind them. Each had their belongings in the tell-tale vinyl bag that was provided. As they stood still, together, and looked out on the newly transformed city, Freddy paced and rubbed his arms, making strange movements with his mouth and teeth. Dominick stood plastically, smoking another cigarette with even, predictable motions.

Before them unfolded a marvel, beyond what either had expected or imagined. It was a city with no advertising, no logos, no mass-produced images of any kind. Not on buildings, not on buses, not on people. All the color was the natural color of living. People's faces were the focus.

It was raining. They stepped forward into a wet, slicked, muted city with no pictures of life, only real life. They saw the red of car lights and a sacred purposefulness in the movements of the people, briskly careening. There were no fake humans doing fake things to sell products. Every image was real.

Dominick wondered if his cigarette was done. Then he wondered how many other cigarettes were still waiting in the pack. He decided to hold off until he heard a human voice before checking his pack one more time. Then he heard a passerby say "ouch," but decided to wait a bit longer anyway. The dread of dealing, of feeling, without having enough cigarettes, was so overwhelming that he could not take in the changes all around.

Freddy, however, was enthralled.

The two different brothers looked at each other and then turned down the block, together, tramping off to their new apartment.

The fact that these two conflicted men could have had fairly humane and effective drug treatment and then walk away, in the rain, to an assigned apartment, was amazing. It seems reasonable, but it had always been unattainable unless the person in question could pay through the nose. But, through the miracle of politics, all the services had been provided. In the old days, they would have never gotten off their drug habits, and would be copping on the street in a matter of minutes, with nothing else to look forward to except that familiar, engrossing hustle. A home would have been an impossibility.

Now, though, with THE CHANGE, these boys had everything going for them that society was newly capable of giving. They still had to provide the hope, but that's why they had each other.

Their new apartment cost sixty-five dollars a month. Each brother had his own chair and his own bed. They shared a bedroom, kitchen, and bathroom. There was a long window at the foot of each bed, and when Dominick slid down, slowly, onto his and smoked a cigarette, he looked out over his shoes at the window. A permanent television set. There was a tree out there, and it was moving. The branches were singing. The rain slid off the leaves. It was always changing. He lay there for years, watching the leaves age, revive. The snow would rest on the branches, and then ten new buds, and then a new green.

While Dom stared, Freddy paced back and forth, fearing the effects of a cup of coffee and hating himself for not being able to appreciate being alive.

"I feel that deep inside myself I am right," Freddy said. "Therefore I am trapped. Because if I thought I was wrong, I could change and avoid being slapped."

"Right about what?" Dominick stared. He didn't get it.

But Freddy was too upset to answer. Any attempted clarification would fail to hit the nail on the head, and he did not ever again want to say anything without fully believing every dimension of it.

"Right about the fact that you are not wrong?" Dominick suggested as he puffed.

"Yeah," Freddy answered, crying over the stove. "Don't ever leave me." Fred's grief was his only self. "I love you so."

Long before this moment, Fred realized that if he were ever to betray Dominick, he might have a normal life. He could have all those rewards that people get for letting their brothers down, for avoiding the Black Sheep. He knew exactly how that process worked. As long as he allowed Dominick to be the Black Sheep on his own, Fred could be superb. If he worked at it, he could have all the status Dom lacked. But Fred would have to collude with everyone else's attitude of disdain towards his only brother. Cluck-cluck, stab in the back, exclude, and condemn—that sort of thing. Then he, Freddy, would be considered superior by all. Not only did his father want it that way, everyone else did too. The bribery was incredible. They begged him to be better than Dom. But Fred stood by his brother because he needed someone to stand by.

Now, with this New Way of Life, the rest of the city was following Freddy's lead. They were officially standing by each other too. Look at this great apartment! It only existed because others cared. And yet, Freddy also knew that a social structure couldn't do all the work of being humane. It could only make a suggestion. Individuals still had to be nicer in order for it to work. Someone still had to sit with a lonely person in a stark apartment holding his hand while the two of them, together, stared out the window.

If Freddy had been someone's wife, others would have considered that kind of loyalty to be the highest virtue. But when it's your brother, you're supposed to throw him to the wolves so that you are free to hold the hand of your lovely wife. Why is a wife better than a brother? Fred did not make up any false, self-justifying theories about why he chose his real brother over a nonexistent wife. He knew the real reason. Fred chose Dominick because his brother was the only true witness to Fred's real history. His true cause.

Only Dominick had seen Fred's real experience and stared it in the face.

No one else could ever know him, and Freddy wanted to be known.

19. SELL ME YOUR RIGHTS

Sophinisba had some explaining to do, and she eschewed television as a way to meet the peeps. She would rather repeat something she believed, over and over again to people's faces, than to say it once in a slick and impersonal way. So Madame Mayor set up a little store-front office and invited the neighbors to stop by for a chat.

The citizens, not being used to this method, were not stopping by in numbers sufficient to be effective, so she moved outside and sat in front of the subway at a little folding table, hoping to catch the folks on their way to THE MEDIA HUB.

"Hey you," she would shout, showing everyone how much she wanted to communicate. Once they realized what was going on, people stopped off for a few minutes and had a mayoral chat. It was refreshing.

Nadine and I happened to pass by one morning while Sophinisba was on an explanation junket. Of course, we stopped to talk, since we liked her so much. We thought she was doing a great job. I mean, we both felt that way at the beginning. I still loved Sophinisba, but at this point Nadine was feeling suspicious about everything in life, including the government.

"Sophinisba is still doing good stuff," I said. "Everyone can see it."

"Well," Nadine murmured. "I don't know."

She was being crabby.

"Ms Mayor?" she said, as we approached the card table where SB presided. "There is something I do not understand."

"That's why I'm here," Sophinisba smiled encouragingly as she simultaneously ran the city through her Finger Pilot.

"All these great changes, all these services. All these humanitarian transformations, Lady Mayor ..." Nadine inhaled. "They cost money! And yet you have dismantled all corporate megaculture from the city's streets. So tell me, how are you paying for all this?"

"Well," Sophinisba gleamed, seemingly ecstatic that someone was paying attention and not just passively receiving. "What a great question." She offered each of us a glass of fresh-squeezed peach juice. "You see, taxing the rich, etcetera, etcetera ... while a great idea, is a concept from a less complex past."

This relieved Nadine, and she dropped her guard. She did not identify with the rich, nor did she want to protect them. But the idea of building a better society by taxing the rich and using their money to help the poor was not a new idea. And this era was supposed to be brand spanking new only.

"Taxing the rich," Sophinisba continued from under her wired pink-brimmed hat. "This can no longer work for a couple of complex reasons."

"Like what?" Nadine asked.

"Basically, the rich would never allow it." Sophinisba shrugged the inevitable. "History has proven this."

We both nodded.

"The rich would rather destroy the universe's atmosphere, beat others to death, starve and humiliate all living creatures, and poison the water supply, than use their extra cash to help others. It just ain't gonna happen."

Nadine was completely impressed. I could tell by the way her lips softened, and her tongue darted in and out.

"And the other reason it can't work ..." A couple of people started hanging around listening. It was getting kind of interesting having a mayor lay it on the line. "... is that the poor are too disorganized to force such a thing. Historically, they have only been able to make progressive change temporarily, usually with the aid of some former prince or kid who went to Harvard. It just never pans out in the long term. The obstacles are too tough. Would you like some pink chocolate?"

We all had two pieces each, all forty of us gathered by the entrance to the Free BMT. It was good, like red chocolate milk. Calm and relaxing and somewhat narcotizing.

All the way to work, Nadine and I talked over Sophinisba's message.

Redistribution of the wealth was a solution from another time. That was true. And therefore, impossible. One of the most long-lasting effects of long-term rapid fire marketing on the New York psyche was that anything that smacked of a previous moment was no longer palatable. Like last month's egg. Unless it was nostalgic. But Retro-Socialism hadn't yet been reintroduced in designer colors. So far, the only thing that Capitalism couldn't contain was Socialism. But everyone knew that it would find a way. Perhaps this was it.

Lenin had promised that the Capitalists would sell us the rope with which we hang them. But he was wrong. The Capitalist sells us the rope with which we hang ourselves. It's direct marketing. No middle-man.

Feeling toasty, with the sweet and sticky chocolate in our guts, we floated off, soothed by the personal touch and reasonable explanation. And yet, that night Nadine woke up angry and afraid.

"What is it, my hon-bun?" I asked, moved by her quantity of emotion.

"How is she paying for this?" Nadine asked. Terrified that she had been deterred.

"Well, she told us, didn't she?"
"What did she say?"
And I could not, for the life of me, remember.

20. OBSCURE or RETIRED?

HARRISON AND CLAIRE were out on a date.

Claire had read the eight words in that week's *Brand New York* about Glick, the country's most unknown artist, and she was impressed that Harrison knew about her when everyone else did not. They went for a walk together to stare at Glick's front door.

Harrison knew, from reading all eight of my pages that none of her work had ever been reproduced, and that none existed in any collections, museums, galleries, or display cases, private or public. It was not in a single lobby or living room. This fact actually haunted him. It was such an extreme example of his worst fear. The fact that it had actually occurred meant it could happen to him. Obscurity. When Claire requested that they view Glick's art, he had to fortify himself with a bottle of Bombay. But then they both arrived and stood, staring, at that sad, horny front door.

Standing there, facing his fears, Harrison realized that despite both her inadequacy and her superiority, he was in love with Claire.

Ginette would never have understood the extreme terror represented by Glick's front door.

Through the window they saw a deranged woman, smoking. Then they returned to the door.

"Well," Claire said after a long sad silence. "It's not very new."

"No," Harrison agreed. "The style is forty-eight years old, at least."

They nodded, knowingly. In unison.

"Of course ..." Claire inserted her hand, and her idea, into

Harrison's pocket. "Old is ... not necessarily ... terrible. Is it? I mean, it won't sell, that's for sure. But this isn't ... isn't for sale, I guess. Right?'

"Don't be naïve," Harrison guffawed. "If Madonna Ciccone wanted to buy this, I'm sure that Glick would sell."

"Madonna" was now an iconic word, like "Jesus." It had no material base. When people said "JESUS!" they did not mean the son of God. They meant an emotion reflecting frustration or astonishment. It had no substance behind it. No person. Saying "Madonna" was like saying "well." The real person had disappeared from public view long, long ago. She might have been dead, or worse, retired. Her name was now a phrase that represented the secret, ultimate desire of every ambitious person. It was an emblem of a crassness so brilliant and calculated that it was beyond reproach.

Harrison and Claire stood for a moment contemplating Madonna as the irrefutable potential corrupter of Glick's pretentious obscurity.

"I don't want to be too conceptual," Claire added sincerely, wearing a cardboard codpiece and plastic diaphragm skirt, "but I do think that the idea behind selling out was that you would change what you made to suit the buyer. Not that the buyer would happen to want to purchase it, as is. Do we condemn people for that now too?"

"Of course not," Bond reassured her. "But if someone has a buyer without having to make changes, then their original concept was commodifiable enough in the first place. They were born selling out. It is the gracefulness of adjustment by which we measure an artist's maturity."

He was thinking of himself. He had never had to sell out, just sell. Harrison went to a college where his parents paid $40,000 a year so that he could ease into the ruling cog. His teachers had gone to the same school and so they identified with him, their younger self. They phoned their other friends from the good old days and told them that their new discovery, Harrison Bond, was exactly like them too. He went to a corporate graduate school to which his parents signed over an additional $80,000, and there he had even more influential teachers who also looked like him. It was a world of people who looked in the mirror but thought it was the window.

This higher tier of teachers phoned their agents and editors who also looked, walked, talked, lived, and wrote like Bond. He drank with them. His book was like theirs. When the publisher bought it, he paid him back the amount of his two tuitions. That kept the money circulating in the right places. By this time, the other guys from the same schools had taken over the major magazines and newspapers. They reviewed his book favorably, with *gravitas*, and wrote feature stories about his *gravitas* as well. He became known for his *gravitas*. Americans did not resemble Harrison and his cronies, but they were used to following orders from people like him, so they did what they were told and bought the book.

Okay, it had happened this way once. It had been incredibly easy, though Harrison thought it was hard. But could he do it again?

Harrison realized, right then and there, standing next to Claire, staring at Glick's eternal failure, that success could only repeat if he didn't worry about it. If he worried, it wasn't success. He had to second-guess nothing. He had to remember that his natural self was exactly what they wanted. The crucial error would be to alter a single gene. He was already perfect. He just had to stay that way.

"But, honey," Claire said, oblivious to the volumes of monologue going on inside him, "Glick never sold anything, remember?"

"Mmmmm," he mmmmed.

"So you really can't put her down for selling out. Right?"

"Guess not," Harrison agreed by negation.

"How strange," Claire bobbed, as they turned away and continued on to a shop. "If everyone thought like her, I'd be out of a job."

"So would they," Harrison laughed suddenly. He was a good sport after all. Someone was more pathetic than he and always would be. This was a fact he must never forget.

21. THE TWO SIDES: IN AND OUT

"YOU KNOW," Nadine said about sixteen times the next day, "we still don't understand where she is getting the cash."

We were strolling on a Sunday a.m. looking at shops. There were so many to choose from. There was the Checkbook Shop, the Dreydel Shoppe, the Wrist Massage Palace, the Imported Ginger Store, and the Allergy Supply Wholesalers, which specialized in different-colored tissues. There was a store where you could pay a small fee to take a nap. Oh look, the Pink Chocolate Spot. That must be where Sophinisba got hers. There were so many to choose from. Each unpredictable from their exterior. Each under no pressure, because their overheard was so low.

"Isn't it weird?" I said. "We used to be able to tell what a store sold by glancing at it, while whizzing by on a bike. Now I have to go all the way inside to figure it out. Walking down the street is like going to a museum. You really need time to look."

We stopped at the Chapstick Store, and then the Chaps Store, next to the Chopstick Spot, the Stick Stock, and the Chicken Stock Shop.

"It's the lack of homogeneity," Nadine surmised. "There won't ever be too many shops selling paper clips, so we won't get used to them and take them for granted. No assumptions. Every moment has to be thought through on its own terms."

People who used to run Subway franchises had the toughest time adjusting because they weren't used to thinking of anything for themselves. Now they had to think of it all. But when your whole society believes that you can do it, well … anything is possible.

"This is going to change my field forever," Nadine gasped. And stood frozen on the sidewalk. "Reliable visual codes, built up over generations soaked in advertising, have simply disappeared. That shared global language of imperial banality. It's gone. "

"Graphic design," I shrieked. "Where is it?"

We both looked up at the sky for some sign of conformist globalized control. But there was only a cloud.

"But, honey, you are still busy at THE MEDIA HUB, right?"

"Busier than before," she said, confused.

"Well, what are you doing there all day?"

"I'm doing what I always did. I'm designing more web pages and cyber ads than ever."

This dichotomy was becoming really mysterious.

We both looked twisted, as when both parties are thoroughly confused, and their two sets of eyes fly around in contrary directions.

"I've got it!" Nadine was so calm. All her wrinkles faded as her face profoundly relaxed. It was as though she had found the secret of Zen.

"What?"

She looked carefully around her.

"There are no more purchasing codes on the street."

"What? What is it? Nadine? Nadine?"

She was twirling, twirling round and round. She was looking, looking, really seeing our grave new world.

"I know what Sophinisba is doing." She was wide-eyed, now. Frantic. Amazed. It was like she had seen the Virgin Mary's leaking blood on a venetian blind. "She hasn't eliminated advertising, or chain stores, or brand names, or franchises."

"She hasn't?"

"No."

"So, where are they?"

"They're inside," she said. "She moved all advertising so that it only takes place intimately. In our private space. Inside. It comes to us at home and at work and through the many, many shifts of mail. Sophinisba flipped it. She flipped it. She made marketing personal, and individuality the common ground. The whole thing has been turned around."

Nadine was right. That was the deal that Sophinisba had ultimately cut with the Richies. No more advertising in public places. But in return she handed them the private sphere on a silver moon. Now we were all theirs.

WOW.

Spending money was now what we did at home. When no one was looking. This stuff on the street was fluff. A diversion.

We were marketed to at work, where we felt employed.

But once we stepped outside of the office, there was none of it. Not a trace.

Sophinisba had realized that the most traumatic and marking things in a person's life happen in secret, in private. They often involve cruelty from someone you love or at least know. All of us are used to this. We don't like it, but it's now familiar to suffer indignities, to be dehumanized and lied to at home. For many of us, life has been that way since childhood. Then we grow up, love someone, trust them, and they hurt us. Again, AT HOME. We know nothing else.

Given this very common but unacknowledged truth, the violation of marketing is just another slap in a very full face. Assimilable.

But public, that's another story. That is a place of display, and trust.

Now, we go home to cry. And to shop.

"WOW," I said filled with love. "My girlfriend is so smart and so wide."

And I took Nadine home, to the marketplace, so that we could make love in private, where everyone was watching.

22. NEWDLE

Harrison and Claire walked around looking for a place to eat. They passed a couple of new schools that Sophinisba had constructed, seemingly overnight. These schools had everything: ten kids in a class, swimming pools, free books.

"YOU NAME IT."

That was Sophinisba's School ReThinking Slogan.

She had invited movie stars to each buy a school district. The place would be named after them and increase that old Benjaminian AURA—how we feel about a movie star when he is offscreen, and how much more that makes us feel about him when he is back on. Also, this was a whole lot easier than having to go to some African country and miss all the parties. Plus, if the star came from a normal background, they could buy the public school in their old neighborhood and really rub it in everyone's face.

Being naturally vicious competitors, the movie stars tried to outdo each other with caring. The Helen Hunt School had free yoga classes, and The Philip Seymour Hoffman School had free bicycles and free glasses.

Then Sophinisba applied the idea to hospitals. She leased them out for brand underwriting to credit card companies.

People adapted quickly. The word on the street soon was that if you were shot, you should go directly to Visa. But, in case of a heart attack or the need for microsurgery, make sure the ambulance took you to Mastercard. A lingering illness was best treated at Discover.

Different cards for different ailments. It helped differentiate them in the consumer's mind. The brands could further distinguish themselves while raising the ante. And they saved money, because it was cheaper to provide quality medical care than it was to buy ad space. This was another revolutionary step in Life Marketing, a newly evolving field. If companies simply ran daily life, that was advertising enough. They didn't need theme songs too.

Consumers didn't have to shift their thinking very far. They had always used credit cards to feel better about not having enough money—and as a way to pretend that inflation wasn't happening. Now, credit cards still made them *feel* better, but they also made them *be* better. Credit cards were healing. It was a brilliant social contract and fantastic psycho-sell.

The first restaurant that Claire and Harrison chose to explore was yellow, with tiny sparking crystal eyes pasted to the windows. Nothing about this decorative strategy conveyed that the place had only three tables and served three kinds of noodle soup. That was it. If you wanted a salad first, you had to go to the salad place, then wander back over here. It was cheap and good, and it was fun. The owner sat in the corner, reading her most recent mail shipment. Her daughter was sitting at the third table doing her homework. It was so humane. The girl's Teach-Shirt said *Henry Louis Gates Public School #4*. He had recently become a big movie star.

"I guess I'll have the noodle soup," Harrison said suavely.

"Oh, I got sick of that stuff." The owner confessed like she was in group therapy. "I couldn't look at another noodle without feeling trapped. Today we are only serving mashed potatoes. Hot, sweet, buttery, salty mashed potatoes."

"Yum," Claire said. "But how can your clients become acclimated to the predictability of your product?"

"Can't," the woman slouched. She was an old-fashioned type of waitress, like in the old movies when they were played by Shelley Winters and not Cameron Diaz. "But then again, unpredictability is the market hook these days. It makes people feel WILD and FREE. Besides, my quality of life improves if I can try new things on a whim. Potatoes?"

"Okay," they said, persuaded, and feeling roguish and unkempt.

It was fun, Harrison realized, being together with Claire in New York, trying new little out-of-the-way places. It was fun being influenced by other people's eccentricities, marginality, and concepts.

Product consistency was just one of Claire and Harrison's many, many shared interests. Then there was an intimate, scary silence.

"Hey," Harrison said, adolescently, his voice cracking. "Did you ever see Andy Warhol's *Drizzle*?" (Andy Warhol never made a movie called *Drizzle*.)

"Yeah," Claire said. "It was great. Isn't that the one with Jon Voigt?" (She's thinking of *Midnight Cowboy*, which was a John Schlesinger Hollywood flick that used Warhol superstars in a party scene.)

Dinner was served.

"Wait, I'm having an insight." Harrison made fun of himself for the first time in years as he dug into his potatoes. (They were fingerling and purple.)

"Tell me," Claire wrinkled her nose in a way that conveyed her cuteness.

"It's about the word *new*. You know ..." He looked at her for acknowledgement and she nodded. YES! YES! SHE UNDERSTOOD WHAT HE MEANT! Gleefully and with a full heart, Harrison continued. "No one ever says: 'Oh, that book is written like Balzac, it's not new.' So why should a painting go out of date with the same speed as a car?"

"The art market?" Claire guessed. "I mean, everything is accelerated now, not just taste. Even emotions have speeded up." She also loved the potatoes. "Too bad that there are not thousands of Glicks instead of thousands of people working on the global Twinkie market. But most paintings are made by one person, right?"

"Unless they are successful and have assistants."

"Right, but most of them don't, right?"

"Right."

"So," Claire said, "a thousand painters equals a thousand paintings. But a thousand marketers equals one Twinkie."

"Emotionally…" Harrison's mind was humping now. "I can look at a painting made even thirty years ago, and if I am not one of the five … oh … three thousand people who are totally up-to-date on the art world, I might actually love it BECAUSE I know nothing. It might be new to *me*."

"Individual Exposure," Claire recalled from an ad she had designed for sheer underpants. "What a concept: each person learning about things one at a time instead of the entire city finding out about the new Snapple flavor at the same minute. It creaks, but it could work."

"What is the new Snapple flavor?" Harrison asked.

"Watercress."

"I love you," Harrison smiled. And regretted it the moment he said it.

23. HONEYBUNNY

I COULD NO LONGER deny that something profound was troubling Nadine.

Unfortunately, it seemed to be me.

I had to take stock. Firstly, there is no such word as "firstly." Second, all my perceptions were turning out to be wrong. This had become abundantly clear. Nadine realized stuff and therefore I admired her. That, apparently, was not good enough.

This fact contributed to my ongoing revelation that I must be an asshole, because all day long at work, and at home, I read on the Cyberscam about other people who I had never met or heard of benefiting tremendously from THE GREAT CHANGE (the new name for what used to be known as the Big Change.) Somehow, because of my many inadequacies, I was unable to access any part of the group betterment for myself and my gal. I couldn't even meet anyone who had managed to do it, even though they appeared to be everywhere.

Opportunity was passing before me.

Who could love a person who missed their historic moment? It was like being a nineteen-year-old college student at Berkeley in 1968 and majoring in Accounting. Or a lesbian in 1979 who decided to go into a convent. A total doofus.

But why? Why couldn't I download my own slice of tolerance?

Ironically, and yet typically, as I resolved to surrender all hope, my true love Nadine was making a contrary decision. We were both on the right road, but I was going in the wrong direction, and she wasn't coming along for the bum steer. No, no swamp for that bright star. Nadine had been making changes.

Her hands may have been callused from entering data, but her mind was on lines—thin pencil and paint. One day, late coming home from work, she announced that she had made a pilgrimage to Glick's front door. She'd stared and stared, transfixed.

Then Glick opened.

Imprisoned in her own bewildered, lonely obscurity, Glick welcomed this kind of visitor. Nadine bragged like a swan about being in Glick's presence, how she had tasted clay and poured cement. She'd used the rest of her body—not just fingers, wrists, and retinas, to make art.

As she regaled me with her triumph, I sat in the bathtub, self-critically, and soaked.

I was worried.

Was Nadine changing her values? And if so, would it be without mercy?

Would it be one of those meat cleaver transformations where anyone who knew the old self had to be destroyed? The kind that made no sense? You know, the cruel kind? Where one kills the other as a symbol of her newly disliked former self?

Or would Nadine come freshly to the table, newly happy with herself and therefore freshly accepting of the world, i.e., me?

"I want to be a painter," she said. "I found a studio today."

"Yay!" I said. "Jubilee!"

"I'm tired of just reading theory. Whee!"

She was smiling. Peace would prevail.

I was relieved. I had never understood why Nadine liked reading theory. It seemed like a substitute for action. How could reading about a painting make it okay not to paint one? I looked at theory once, and it seemed to be a kind of subtle but convoluted way for people to explain why they and their friends should be the ones in charge.

Once again our life grew and deepened out of a crisis, as Nadine expanded her personal vision, and, I hoped, her tolerant love for little old me. It wasn't instability envy, just that not knowing what is going to happen makes people strange and frightened if they want something very, very much. Something very big. Bigger than the usual human allotment. So, as Nadine grew into her painterly role, I looked in the mirror constantly. Everybody else seemed to have an assignment from fate. But I had to create my own homework. Because the errors never ceased.

"You're not going to quit your job, are you?" I squeaked in terror.

So much for my good intentions.

Immediately, I saw by her expression that I had made a gross error. I seemed trite and unimportant, with no clue as to what really counts. Whoooooopsie, wrong strategy. People dump you for less. Oh my God, is there nothing worse than saying the wrong thing? My level of insecurity informed me of how much danger I was in. I mean, it's not like we had just started dating. I should have shouldered her disapproval as a temporary bump.

"I mean, I mean … I mean … I was thinking about getting some more stability. I mean, some stability."

"Well," she scorned, black hair glowing thick and juicy as an oil spill. "You know that my cat is named Cotton Mather, and that I both love my certainty and am used to it. But now I want even MORE. I want to pull myself up by my bootstraps and at the same time be a trapeze artist, happily flung to my net."

"But there is no net," I cried.

Oy vey. To err is human, so what's my excuse? I built my own scaffold and tried on the noose.

"Listen," I said in my girlfriendly way. "You're right, Nadine, and I am wrong. Protection only comes from within, I guess. And yet, I also feel that the attentive mob might actually be illusory. They can turn as quickly as the night. All we have is each other, I guess." These were my facts and fears laid out like a cadaver. Or a gift.

"I'll think about it," she lied. For the rest of the night she read a book, as I silently watched commercials and worried.

24. THE AGE OF SENSE

UNBEKNOWNST TO ME, the book Nadine was reading that night, *The Age Of Innocence*, was set in Manhattan in the 1870s. Central Park was a wilderness then, surrounded by one-story saloons and hills topped with goats. Rich people whispered through the opera, which they had to go to Fourteenth Street to see. They noticed no one but each other.

. It was a delicious book. Edith Wharton pulled through all her tropes.

Newland Archer, her hero, loved the main female character, May, principally because she was acceptable. However, she turned out to be a fairly deep person, despite her obedience. They announced their engagement at the ball. Later, Newland fell in love with the wrong woman, someone who would ruin his life because the exterior punishment of being with her would, mathematically, outweigh all personal satisfactions. But because choosing her would mean that he was a man who preferred satisfaction, he would have to leave her when the punishments overtook them. It was a Catch-22.

If he stayed with the acceptable and really kind of cool lady, he could anticipate a different type of satisfaction in the long run. He would enjoy some version of it, no matter how temperate.

At this point, Newland pushed the acceptable one to marry him faster because he wanted to make the possibility of being with the wrong woman something from the past. He wanted to eliminate the option.

His fiancée guessed this. He was afraid to admit her suspicions because he was afraid that she would punish and humiliate him, deprive him, and send him off on the wrong path. But she did not.

She asked him honestly what he felt, and she let him speak the truth.

This strategy was disarming and dangerous. It made him feel accepted and understood despite his inappropriate but true emotions.

It made him pass up profound satisfaction followed by long-term despair for a mild acceptance on an even keel. His fiancée did him a favor.

But then she blew it with her stupid, petty jealousy, and he was alone again with his desire.

25. NADINE'S SOLILOQUY

I, NADINE, HAVE no sympathy for Newland Archer, or any other creep who wants it both ways. You can only have it one way on this earth. Only the perfect can ask for forgiveness and get it, the rest had better shut up. I'm too busy.

My girlfriend, the "author" of this despicable, unforgiving book you are currently reading instead of Edith Wharton (don't you feel foolish?) is a real jerk.

Look at the way she knows what every character is doing and feeling, even when she is not in the room. That's just wrong. Any teacher of fiction knows that much.

I have figured out how to make THE BIG CHANGE work for me. By example. The society changed, so I can too. That's how it works. The society doesn't change FOR me. I have to watch and then do it for myself.

If you examine it with any pith, this New Society is really still for the same people who ran the Old Society. Why can't my girlie figure that out? It is what Herbert Marcuse called "repressive tolerance." They make you feel freer so that they can get more control. Why doesn't she understand?

Actually, I can see some startup glimmers in her otherwise dusty eyes, some beginning realizations that things are not going to work out her way. But she only realizes this subconsciously.

I know, before we go to bed, that we are out of milk.

But she only finds out once the hot coffee is in the cup.

Then she stands, stupidly, before the opened refrigerator door, in her dragonfly pajamas, cup in hand and finally, AND ONLY THEN, is she disappointed. I was disappointed all night.

GET WITH IT!

Knowledge is available a lot sooner than you think.

Lately, the first thing she says after any long period of silence is: "Why is this happening to me?"

And EACH TIME I answer: "You cannot ask me this every single day."

I mean, life is tough, but so what?

What right did she have to expect justice anyway?

What's the point of suffering for having been stupid?

Just be smart, and you'll feel better.

Believe me, more than once I have just blurted out: SHUT UP AND GET A BETTER JOB OR ELSE STOP COMPLAINING.

My idea is that she try to climb at THE MEDIA HUB. She's been writing ad copy since first grade. It's time for her to conceptualize ad copy, not just write it out. She needs goals.

On the other hand, I am not a monster. I understand how all this unfolded. When things were officially terrible, she knew the score. But when things improved, she never adjusted.

It stinks, but it's a fact. There comes a time when you have to choose between surgery and suicide.

As they say at work, *You can't play a laser disc if there is no electrochip.* Know what I mean?

Let me simplify this into more nostalgic terms so that you can get it. You can't play a record if there is no electricity. You can't play a record if there are no record players. You can't play a record if they don't make records any more. It may not be right, but it is happening. So, MOURN, MOURN, MOURN your old expired self. Then be done with it.

You lost, you silly butch. Everything's better, so it's a different game now.

GET A BETTER JOB.

26. CITIZENSHIP CUMMARY

IN THE UNIVERSE of this novel, *The Mere Future*, here is a recap of where we all stand.

NADINE AND I
We are equally in love and equally not. There is no accurate measure. A hand on a wrist. That beautiful face. Its limits become one of those ultimate mysteries.

HARRISON AND CLAIRE
The room was so crowded with their sadness. A simple sigh would have collapsed it. They glance, a narrow road. Hearts pounded or stopped. No difference between grief and collapse. Impossible demands. Another signifying the existence of truth.

HARRISON AND GINETTE
They shared details of the day at work. Each one knowing all the other's characters. The other's details. The other's predictable reactions, a second skin. Each other's taste in wire baskets, sauce, streams, shows. All known. Remember the blue hills? Remember the stapler? Remember the vault?

CLAIRE AND JEFF
If life was based on feelings, it would all be clear. But propriety brilliantly obstructs. And so they behave and revert to private torments whose existence the other tearfully doubts. Scenarios replayed privately by the memoirist alone in a chair. The room is lack, the radio

strums. Pleasure, interior and recalled.

JEFF AND HIS SON FRED

Exhausted limitations, division exhausted. Refusals both low-grade and the highest tar. No effort. No satisfaction.

JEFF AND HIS SON DOMINICK

A heavy satchel dragged from place to place. Subtracting chunks on a daily basis.

FREDDY AND DOMINICK: THE BROTHERS

A bowl of soup, some rain. A shaking—but not of the fist. Gazing irrationally, serene as a drill press that signs the presence of somebody else's progress. Forgotten inventory. Paging through a blank book, a boring book, an old book with no relevance. Rocking as they pursue an understanding of the mountain. Two skies in one day.

LATER THAT SAME ERA

27. INVISIBLE SCAM

JEFF WAS FOLLOWED everywhere by everything he'd ever done wrong. He was paranoid, but that did not energize him. Even with psychotic fear, he felt lifeless. That dichotomy was his clearest evidence that something was profoundly wrong with his life. After all, if he was Death Incarnate, then why was he being chased?

Jeff was frantic with entropy.

He decided to try to relax. But how? TV was no fun these days. It just made him want to buy stuff.

He paced back and forth. Then he realized that holding up the fourth leg of the table that supported the TV was a book. The only book in the house. It was a gift from Claire, but he had never opened its covers. Carefully, Jeff lifted the TV set and placed it on the floor. It was a Fold Screen, so he rolled it under the bed. Then he moved the table and picked up the thick volume with the deep imprint of a table leg in its center. It was by a man named Ralph Ellison.

Jeff started the first page but didn't get it. So he skipped to Chapter Two. It had been so long since he had read an actual book that Jeff had forgotten that you can't just pick up at the second episode and figure out who's who. If it's a GOOD book, you won't ever have met characters like that before. He was pretty frustrated by his inability to figure out what kind of book it was: Domestic Sit-com or Police Drama.

Then, suddenly, like a triple shot of tequila, it overtook his mind. INVISIBLE MAN hit! Reading Chapter Two was like staring into the sun.

Here's why:

In Chapter Two, a rich white man hears that a poor black man has impregnated his own daughter. This fascinated Jeff. Why would someone want to do something like that? It escaped him.

Whitey goes to the sharecropper's house to tell him off, to lecture him on why impregnating his daughter was wrong. But instead of actually explaining it, he starts off the confrontation by asking the black guy why he fucked her.

The black man in question, named Trueblood, then begins a monologue that lasts about twelve pages. He never stops talking. He explains, in his gorgeous, seductive, entertaining, intriguing, juicy way, the slyest feelings and most vulnerable sensual gestures that lead to that crucial morning when he penetrated the girl. His justification is so sexy that the white man forgets entirely about standard protocol. It is intoxicating, the desire these two bandy about. It is completely familiar, casual, and entirely understandable. It is something that men share. In fact, the white man is now so enchanted that he hands Trueblood a one-hundred dollar bill. That's how persuasive Trueblood's story is.

Jeff also was a horrible father. He didn't fuck his children, but he did other things to destroy them. Like Trueblood, he knew that he had done something wrong. But still, he wanted to get away with it. And he enjoyed the escape. He was good at avoiding responsibility, and a person needs to be good at something. Even if it is only denial. It suddenly gave Jeff a sense of self he had never known—to imagine pulling something off, no matter what it was.

It is in this way that readers derive messages from books that have nothing to do with the author's intentions.

Because, actually, Trueblood was ironically and complexly standing up for himself as a black man. The white guy had no right to ask him anything, no matter how gross his misdeed. It was none of the white man's affair. He had no right to walk into this black man's house and quiz his morality. And yet Trueblood could not tell the white guy to fuck off, because he could get lynched. If the reader just focused on this aspect—Trueblood's courageous resistance to white supremacy—then one could forget that he was a child fucker. That was the brilliant trick of the book. And that was exactly how Jeff felt about the Richies, the kind of folks that Claire seemed to rub shoulders with. It made him hate her proximity to them. That was the only thing about her that he hated. But that was a lot.

Further interpreting the book through his own lens, Jeff realized that even though he sucked as a parent, he was still a working-class man, doing a boring hard job. And that gave him some kind of decency. In fact, being exploited was the definition of decency. He did his horrible job instead of pawning it off on others as the Richies did.

Trueblood showed Jeff that he could be a monster and still be okay. Nothing else in his life ever had. Jeff reconsidered books and started to love them. He could pretend they said anything he wanted them to say, and as long as he stayed out of classrooms and book groups, no one would claim otherwise. The only thing that kept him from reading nonstop from then on was the fact that books had come back into style. He didn't want to be like every other fucker. Books were coming back as part of the Low-tech Revolution. Jeff had always known better than to do/believe what everyone did and believed. Trends were all constructed, any idiot knew that. He'd been a computer mechanic for twenty years and he knew how the plastic hearts who ran the world functioned. Those plasties. They'd come up with some slogan like:

to sell an antihistamine that caused mood swings. After all, everyone was used to psychotic behavior, but no one liked sniffling. The slogan would go out on the psycho-serve for a while, then the magazines would pick it up as a headline to an unrelated article. For example:

"Better Potty Than Knotty"

Which would turn out to be an article about The Boy Scouts and their rope work. Then the TV anchors would just happen to adlib it a couple million times, and before the new sun rose, it was plastered all over Teach-Shirts. A week from Thursday, he would be having a fight with Claire, and in their most private, intimate moment, she'd rhyme something with *potty*. The ad had become their life.

Claire. It had been three months since she'd dumped him, and he was still carrying a blowtorch.

The level of self-consciousness that the Beats brought to art-making is perhaps their worst legacy. Yet it never trickled up to those who needed it most. A little self-consciousness would sober up those plasties. It used to be easy to identify the establishment and say what a "square" was. Now, who knew? Trends came only from the center. The margins? Where are they?

Jeff looked around himself. Where? Where? He couldn't find a single edge.

There were no real hipsters, just the folks with power and those without. This whole system left people like Jeff out in the cold. And the advertisers claimed "society" had changed—but, except for reading a great book, Jeff's life was feeling worse and worse. There was no place to hide from Competition: The Social Aggression. And it didn't acknowledge its own existence.

Now, with all the mail deliveries, Power Guys could plant stories on the mid-morning, late-morning, and early-afternoon news. They kept reporting that people were going back to reading books because the only thing on the serves, scans, TVs, and glossies were ads, ads, ads. People were saturated, the News said. They wanted some emotional catharsis ... suddenly. And guess what? These reports were ads themselves. The product? Books!

Jeff was tripping on all of this. He stared and mulled. He stepped outside and looked at things differently. He saw that those dressed as trendsetters were walking down the streets reading, feeling free about it. Flaunting their books. He knew that they were probably buying stock in book companies, automatically, as they walked. This made them double-cool—and richer.

Jeff was sure that books were another invented fad. They stunk of it. He recalled the good old days when trends started in someone's living room and happened to catch on. Those days were long gone. But that's the price everyone has to pay if they want low rents. Right?

Jeff hated himself. He could have pulled out his own beard. That's how sad he was. He'd spent the last three months smashing his fists down on his own skull and still he deserved more punishment. He'd fucked up the whole thing with Claire. Claire. Claire. Claire. Claire. And it was all over those stupid letters she'd sent him. He should have just appreciated them. He should have just kept them happily, as a sign that someone loved him once, even if not enough. But, instead, he had to over-interpret. He didn't know. He didn't know that lots of people spoke so intimately to lots of other people at the same time. He was terrified.

How was Jeff to know that all around him people were sharing intimacy as if it were nothing? They were sharing praise and what they appreciated about each other, what they loved about each other. He had no idea that that was normal—to own the love that you feel. How could he? He'd rather kill her than have that happen. Rereading those letters made him want to fuck her again. But when he told her so, she didn't want to. Then she said that she did think he was sexy, but that relationships are about more than two people. They're also about the world. And, while she was sure that he would be so kind and loving to her on a personal level, she didn't think that the relationship would work "socially."

Claire let him go.

Socially? SOCIALLY?

SOCIALLY?

He wasn't fucking society. He was fucking her.

That's why Jeff loved Trueblood, because Trueblood did what he had to do, and then he could explain it. Of course, those were the days before the twenty-four-hour Incest Channel. Ladies with big hair from Milwaukee came on around-the-clock and told how their parents' Satanic cult committed ritual abuse. They described how their mothers poked their vaginas with knitting needles, killed babies, and made their daughters eat the livers of the dead babies before boarding alien space ships.

Jeff never wanted to take one step out of Manhattan. Here, when people kill their own children, there is no Martian involved.

He preferred the Defense of Incest Channel, where men with expensive haircuts, and also some regular Joes, defended their rights to rape their children. They believed that the bad Puritans wanted to ruin everything.

Anyway, there was a lesson to learn from Trueblood. Even after three months, Jeff could win back Claire's love, SOCIALLY, if only he could become persuasive.

28. MAIL

DOMINICK QUIETLY tended the bonfire out back behind the store. That's how he spent his days now. He'd wake and smoke a cigarette, lying in bed in his undershorts while Freddy cooked up a bowl of oatmeal. Then they would walk across the street to their store and make some coffee. Then Dominick would light up another smoke.

They liked their store.

Freddy loved to sit at the front desk and wait for dispatchers to come in. Then he'd pay them by the bag.

It had not taken many days of apartment living in The New Era for the brothers to start paying attention to the mail. It came at least five times a day, often more. Each time, their box would be full. But Fred and Dominick didn't have any friends, nor were they doing any business. Besides the occasional postcard from their counselor, Ginette, their mailboxes were stuffed to the brim with ads.

At first, Freddy dutifully brought the stacks of paper into the house with regularity. Some of them had nice pictures and designs and others had special smells, sounds, and textures related to specific products. But the paper quickly overtook their lives. They tried pasting layers of it onto the walls as decorations, but soon the size of their apartment was greatly diminished. Freddy made some shelves out of it, but soon the shelves overflowed with mail. That's when Freddy got the idea of opening up a dump. Within hours many of their neighbors were paying a small fee to have a dispatcher (Freddy) clean out the stuff on a regular basis, and Dominick's job was to burn it all in a ditch out back.

The ad producers were upset at first by this unforeseen development, but since the number one rule of advertising is that "people and systems act on and transform each other," they quickly recognized that a new market was dawning. So they started producing "Mail Dumper" Teach-shirts, baseball caps, and tote bags, which advertised the wearer's rebellion against the mail system. These new items were first produced in small quantities and sold only in specialty shops, but then they started to appear in knock-off versions and could be purchased through any website. A condom was produced called "The Male Dumper." All needs were met. Before he knew it, Freddy found a newspaper headline trumpeting: MAYOR, A MALL DUMPER, when Sophinisba banned shopping malls from the island of Manhattan. Then some dispatcher mumbled it to Fred when referring to his old lady, never realizing that he was repeating an ad.

It was a crazy autumn day. At first, the big tree out back had slowly revealed a bright orange underbelly and then a kooky red surface. It cascaded into bright gold, which had now become as crispy and brown as a shoe, brown as a single piece of singed mail.

Dominick was quiet, neither constant nor desiring. He was numb. He smoked. He feared any tension. He was self-medicating by staring at the flames. He feared any strong emotions. Fred, on the other hand, loved his job. He loved chatting with the dispatchers, carrying the stacks of paper out back. He loved the way the sacks pulled on the sinew of his back and created unsightly, out-of-character lumps of hard tissue at the same weird points on both arms. He knew from TV that most people paid for their lumps with their lives. They spent every last cent on gym clothes, and then on gyms. They spent their most important years trudging up machines. He knew that there were actually writers, sitting at home, trying to decide between writing a book or going to the gym. When that didn't work, they had plastic surgery. Most New York bodies were extremely expensive. But his was for free. Besides, he could never use those machines. He didn't know how to program.

Having a function blunted his compassion. He had goals now, which prioritized actions and took him outside of the realm of unity with all mankind. He'd had a good idea, and clearly no longer wanted a lover, now that he'd achieved something. No use risking failure when success felt so fine. Why get wrapped up in the promise of a pleasure he wouldn't be able to feel secure about until he was already sick of it? Like his father. Jeff. His father was lovesick for someone he was so mad at, he would have spent the entire relationship getting back at her, or getting her back, if she'd give him either chance. Fred did not want that life. He'd rather burn the mail.

29. LAKE

"That's some fire you've got there."

Dominick didn't even blink. Three or four times a day someone said, "Hey, that's some fire you've got there." It was a sign. A sign of the other person's loneliness or lack of purpose, of a superficial desire to connect without the ability to offer something more. It was a clue of banality, of a person who just repeated what they had heard someone else say. It was a symbol of emptiness or a search for a blank conversation to fill a blank afternoon.

"Son," Jeff said, squatting down next to his son, "that's some fire you got there. You've grown up to be a pretty good fire tender after all."

Oh no, thought Dominick, panicking as a terrible excitement took over his being. His father had returned to destroy him.

"I remember when you were a boy and I took you to a lake. Do you remember?"

Dominick nodded, wishing, wishing, that the old man would go back to ignoring him.

"We did all kinds of things. Right, my son?"

"Right."

"When you were six we went for a walk. When you were seven I took you to the park, remember? They say that the first seven years of a boy's life are the most important. Don't they? Don't they?"

"I don't know," Dominick whimpered.

"They do! Voices carry over lakes. Did you know that? Son? Two fellows can be out on a boat fishing and sharing a couple of secrets and the next thing you know, the women back on shore, unwrapping those tuna fish sandwiches, well, they know every detail. The guys come to land and the little ladies are gone. They packed up the picnic lunch and threw it in the trash. People think that nature keeps their secrets, but it don't. Listen to me, Dom. The old man's got some experiences that can help you out. Let me be the wise old one and you'll have an easier time of it. I'm warning you."

Jeff picked up a perfume sampler and threw it on the fire.

"Now the whole world will smell of perfume," Jeff said. "Ain't that nice?"

Many people before him had made the same assumption, but actually nothing smelled stronger, when it was burning, than ink.

30. TITANIC

WHEN GINETTE finished her lettuce lunch, she settled on a carrot-dipped cucumber for dessert. All day she planned her strategy for how to get out of her second job at the clinic. She was so sick of drug addicts. Sick of doing "good works" for others. Blech. She was sick of checking their rectal cavities, sick of hearing their lies, their pain. She was sick of sitting in offices with people who had wasted a lot or most of their time. And she hated taking care of them because no one else would. They were mostly weak, shafted by the social structure, or had genetic predispositions that were so ingrained, even amputation wouldn't have changed anything. What she really wanted out of life was to climb at THE MEDIA HUB, get a better design job, and have a bit more status in the scheme of things. She wanted to do something with her life that really mattered, like be an Art Director.

For three years Ginette had secretly been working on a master mock-up for a design idea to break into the big time. It was a four-dimensional makeup case with an Indian bedspread motif, chrome plating, and scratch-n-sniff. She knew it was a winner. Every week she sent it out to a different art director and hoped desperately for a reply. To date, she had sixty-five rejections out of 380 submissions. She knew that the other remaining 315 art directors would probably never get back to her. They had already stolen her idea or thrown it away. This was all because she was a nobody and didn't come from the right family. Her father was a shoe salesman and her mother was a CPA. In order to get in with an art director, you needed to have a father who was Idi Amin and a mother who was Peggy Lipton.

But one day, while glancing at the Scan, she saw a spotlight on Nadine, art director at the CAN-BC Autodimension Design Division of THE MEDIA HUB. Ginette recognized her from the street. Nadine had really cool lip gloss. She was gay, and those girls tended to be nicer to Ginette, plus Nadine said, in the spotlight, that she was "open to new dimensions." Ginette sent her a really slick q-mail, and a prototype with an anti-Xerox coating. No point in taking any chances. Nadine called her two minutes later, apologizing for the delay. She said she'd seen Ginette "around" many times, and would "love" to get together. She apologized twice again.

Why is she apologizing when these types are usually real cunts? Ginette thought.

So they got together for water, to talk things over.

"This is the best design I have ever seen in my life," Nadine said. "And I am so honored to be working with you. Let's get together again next week."

"You know," Ginette said at their second meeting, "I had a dream about you."

"I'm so honored to be in your dreams," Nadine said. "Now, let me tell you that I have just been put on retainer by Sophinisba herself to develop a new design for the city crest. If you can turn this makeup case into a city crest, we've got a deal."

"Oh, wow," Ginette said, calculating. She had approached 380 art directors. Nadine was the only one who wanted to rescue her from social work. "It's a deal. Do you think the city crest could be a makeup case?"

"Hold that thought," Nadine said. "Call me on Thursday and we'll set up a meeting."

When Nadine went home that night, she looked at her girlfriend, me. She knew that she loved Ginette in a way that she could never love me. After all, I was there and Ginette was a fantasy. But that if she pursued Ginette, everything would be a disaster. Showing your desire is an invitation for pain.

She had to think it over.

She thought and thought.

Ginette called and called, called and called. She called every day for thirteen months.

Nadine thought and thought. Thought and thought. Finally, Nadine called her back. "I really apologize," Nadine said. "Let's meet four months from Thursday at 1:13."

"Okay," Ginette said. "My house would be fine."

Nadine felt that that extension would give her time to decide.

That day Ginette scrubbed and scrubbed. She needed this job, and no one else had called her back. Ginette spent the last of her paycheck on smoked mozzarella from Pittsburgh, slicing the cheese lovingly, arranging it beautifully on the most precious platter.

Nadine decided at the last minute that this was ridiculous. She had to get rid of me before she started dating someone else. But how? In the meantime, she blew off the date.

This predictable no-show by Nadine created a weird obsession in Ginette's mind, as all withholding always does. All Ginette could think about night and day was why Nadine lied to her. What Nadine had said to her. What Nadine promised her. All the ways Nadine recreationally misled her, and why? Why? Why?

Nadine became her air and water. She couldn't think about anything else except for this chick who'd fucked her over, who'd taken away her dream. As always happened, this kind of hatred was deeply erotic. How else can you feel about the person who has what you want? Who goes out of her way to offer it to you, and then won't show up? It's a cock tease, and it works. Night after night, Ginette tossed and turned in her sweaty little bed, imaging Nadine's luscious body. Fucking her with a tree. Whenever she had sex with a man, Ginette imagined it was Nadine, especially at the moment of pain. She'd walk down the street always looking for Nadine. Every room she entered, she was prepared. Even when her beeper sounded that a client was in trouble, she had her hand around Nadine's neck and her underpants stuffed firmly into Nadine's petulant mouth.

31. THE CITY THAT NEVER LISTENS

RIGHT AFTER THE CHANGE, Sophinisba worried that all shops would cease. Americans had gotten into the habit of ordering items off the Scan. They'd think of what they wanted, tell the Scan, and charge it. Since nothing was made in the US anymore, the computer would order the thing from production plants in the Democratic Republic of Congo and keep the profits. They didn't have to stock inventory or make selections. It was an interesting process that intrigued everybody because they had to rely on their imaginations to understand what they would like. The consumer had to project an image, instead of cathect with a displayed object. And therein lay the fatal flaw.

At first, everyone delighted their own fancy, dreaming up boxes of dried boysenberries and goat milk soufflé, reversible cars, instant intimidation machines, automatic sneaker scrubbers, and see-through jockstraps. But after a while, the rusty imaginations felt taxed. Only Africans knew how to make things, and Americans could barely think. This shopping system required the consumer to constantly come up with something desirable, and this was impossible to achieve with regularity while simultaneously multitasking and doing Pilates. Consumers wanted limits, perfection, parameters of selection.

So, ever responsive, the Scan started providing leading suggestions to make the process less taxing on the consumer. To give her the illusion of creativity without actually having to come up with anything.

For example:

DO YOU WANT SOMETHING:
1. groovy   2. funky   3. tasteful   4. demure   5. kitsch
6. chic   7. hung   8. decent   9. mysterious   10. organic
11. dependable   12. pan-Asian   13. high carb   14. raw

But even that degree of specificity never turned out to meet the consumer's expectations. Most of the items got returned. Shopping was not fulfilling its potential in a world where personality still reared its ugly head. So shops were born again. Shops and books. Ultimately, the market always returns to the basics.

We always return to the basics, Freddy read, heard, and then thought as he watched his father's lying face spewing all that bullshit. Yet, suddenly, something unspeakably cruel happened. Freddy's father stood up, threw up his hands, showed Fred his disgust, and beckoned casually in Dominick's direction.

Shockingly, as Freddy's world fell, Dominick stood mechanically, dusted ash off his pants, and left his brother behind to follow his father down the street.

Fred stared.

Dominick staggered behind Jeff.

How could this happen?

The problem was that Fred had invested his entire heart in a helpless addict who had no resistance. Freddy had depression; that was his resistance. Dominick had no such brakes.

As Fred watched his soul be demolished, Dom did what his father said because he had cravings, cravings that could not be defied. He was addicted to the hope that someday his father would be interested in him, that someday he would have protection and guidance. This was his Jones.

When Fred watched his darling brother going off with Pop, he slowly got moving and lumbered along. He didn't *have* to. It wasn't a compulsion. He followed anyway, because to abandon Dominick, in Dominick's moment of abandoning him, would have been grotesque. Historically, every time Dad let Dominick down, Fred stood by Dom's side. He had promised himself, early on, that only when his father was kind to Dominick would Freddy allow his father to be kind to him too. Paternal love should not be exclusive to one child.

If Freddy had just allowed Jeff to privilege him, while treating Dom like dirt, it would have violated the most sacred relationship on earth. It was the only relationship in Fred's life that was not by coincidence or choice. Fred loved his brother because he was his brother. Not because of what Dom could do for him. This was a relationship of human loyalty, not family currency. And so, Freddy followed them down the block.

"You see, kids," Jeff said obsessively, "Claire always wanted a family of her own."

Oblivious to what his sons were thinking, Jeff was reliving the Claire situation.

"But one day she rented some bench time in the Central Park Mall. As she sat, four hundred couples walked by with little babies in strollers. All of the mothers were over thirty, but dressed like fifteen-year-olds. All of the fathers had pained, hyper-masculine expressions of raw possibility under constraint. All the kids were named Waldo, Cornelius, Theodora, or Lucille. All the kids were going to grow up with enormous entitlement that they did not merit. They would then strive to become Republican super-models. It was pathetic. And so she knew that she could never be a part of it."

Jeff lead his sons down Merrill Lynch Boulevard, across Shearson

Lehman Street, and turned right on J. Crew Avenue. They stopped in front of the National Gym, and boldly jaywalked over to a tiny cinder box of studio duplexes. Then they walked upstairs.

"But OUR family," Jeff continued, "we have nothing prefabricated. We are not conventional. We have no social advantages. Maybe we will fit her needs."

They stood, preparatorily, in front of apartment $E.

"If she could see us all together, she might not be such a snob."

Jeff knocked on the door. Unexpectedly, the balsa slab slid open, and the three men looked in through the narrow doorway.

There was a brief light creeping under the drawn window blinds. And it was surrounding Harrison Bond.

Bond's hands were dripping in blood. He leaned over Claire's mutilated corpse.

"Oh my God," Jeff gasped.

Harrison looked up at the three of them, stricken with capture. He had a floppy, sexy new haircut. He was huge, and his aqua-weave shirt was soaked in gore.

Jeff, Dom, and Freddy looked at Claire's body, splayed out across her living room floor. Her face had been cut open. He torso was slashed.

Harrison clutched a jagged can opener.

Then the three men saw what was actually taking place. Claire's chest had been cracked and pried wide, then her heart had been lifted out of her body. Strangely, though, the attaching muscle had not been severed, so it hung from her body's cavity.

One thing was clear to all. Claire Sanchez would never live again.

Harrison looked at these three panicked men. His fear softened and then passed. He had just been having the greatest feeling of relief that a man can ever experience. His worst fantasy had been fulfilled. Nothing more horrible or more pleasurable would ever take place again. He had finally expressed himself, for real. For the first time in his repressed, angry, frightened life, Harrison Bond had done what he needed most to do.

But now that fleeting perfect happiness, like all happiness, was over because of other people. It was over because Jeff, Freddy, and Dom had walked in on the middle of his release.

Harrison gazed up, still bent over. Having his hand inside Claire's chest was the most intimate he had ever been with another person. The most unpretentious. She could not judge him or lie to him, evade or avoid or blame him for anything. She could not reduce him. This was her heart. There was nothing bullshit about it. It was real.

Harrison's mouth slid open. Saliva fell to the floor. He almost died standing up—from too much excitement.

"You!" Harrison shrieked, pointing a dripping fist at the three smaller men. "How could you do this? You animals!"

32. NO WORLD

No WORLD, Ginette thought, rushing to the holding cell. *No world.*

She wanted it to go away.

There had been many, many times over the course of her years at her second job working with sad people, that her former drug addict clients had relapsed or gotten in trouble of a petty or grandiose kind. That's the nature of sadness. When people are already in trouble, they become easy targets for more.

After all, if a well-dressed, clean man asked you for help, you would be more likely to help him than if he was sick, dirty, and bleeding. But the sick, dirty, and bleeding man would need it more. Right?

Many times, over the years, little Ginette had had to run to clinics and hospitals, jails and morgues. That was routine.

But not these guys. Not those little brothers.

(She was refusing these events.)

No, not *THEM*!

How did sweet, nice sad boys like Dom and Fred get caught up in pain this severe?

Ginette was deeply afraid for the brothers because she knew very well how the system worked. She knew that innocence was irrelevant. Okay, that's a cliché, but still true and disconcerting. And she was sure that they were innocent. They weren't capable of feeling anything deeply enough to lead them to commit a crime of passion.

The Destruction of the Innocent, volume 1,982,103,332, was underway.

Punishment without crime. That's the way of the world. No one can escape.

Nadine said to call, so I called, Ginette reasoned. *And then I got humiliated and sad.* So clearly Dom and Fred were innocent—Ginette had been innocent, after all.

It's so easy to get slammed. Even if you do what they say. What you do has no bearing on the matter. The question is, *Do they need someone to slam?* If they do, you're fucked.

It started out with Nadine and ended up with two scared, tiny men being falsely accused of murder. Plus their father.

That's why, as far as Ginette was concerned, it was big people, art directors like Nadine, who should go to jail. Not little-bitty Dommie and Freddie.

People who lie on the small plane are just making the big lies more palatable and harder to resist. That's what Ginette had learned. She had tried to make an alliance with some powerful art director, but instead here she was with the imprisoned shmucks. She had tried to date the popular, the wealthy and connected Harrison Bond. But instead she was running to jail to visit some pathetic, sad people who just wanted to burn garbage and smoke. Her life was not going the right way.

On the street, as she walked toward the prison, she felt so guilty for having had ambitions. How dare she ever try? It was gross the way she was willing to sell out everyone she'd ever met, make them live with a compact and an eyeliner for the city crest. How could she impose that level of tasteless kitsch on all these unsuspecting hard-working New Yorkers passing her innocently on the street?

She arrived at the prison and showed her retina to get in.

Prisons had been more affected by television than by Sophinisba. All those prison and cop shows had prepared America for clean, modern institutions, with articulate and consistent prisoners. Since the people who get convicted for crimes often watch more TV than those who don't, this particular group was particularly disappointed. The putrid, boring, scary wasting of life was nothing like what they showed on *Law & Order*. And this made everybody mad.

As a result, a series of TV riots took place over a number of years. The inmates demanded broadcast-quality conditions. A compromise was reached in which TV backdrops were placed on top of the old rotting cells. This gave each convict a drywall interior pasted up against the rusty iron bars. Somehow that was comforting to viewers of reality TV shows like *Rikers* or *Death Row*, which followed real-life inmates as they did their time, tried to stay alive, traded sex for drugs, and became jailhouse lawyers and Muslims.

The networks installed huge-screen monitors so prisoners could watch each other sleep on props and eat props every week. It made them feel romantic, important, and somewhat fantastical. This sedated them. The unreal feeling of punishment was surrounded by the Real Unreal. Everything was truly fake. This made incarceration more tolerable.

Ginette, used to visiting clients in the clink, got through the various checkpoints without much problem. The people hired to search visitors were themselves using and selling drugs, so they didn't do a tip-top, thorough job of searching her shoes. After a few checkpoints and two metal detectors, she made it to the holding pen.

"What does all this mean, officer?"

Ginette flashed her counselor's badge, and so the cop had to talk to her with some intent. The two women were standing in the narrow concrete hallway, looking into the cell where Freddy, Dom, and Jeff were imprisoned. They all looked deader than usual. Calm. As though the outside had finally matched the inside. They were terrified and tortured, tormented. But they always had been. Now, it was justified—caused by the world around them and not just their father and paltry interior lives. This justified unhappiness created a tiny sense of calm.

"Look," Officer Perez told Ginette, while secretly admiring her compact case. "Having personally run electrotropes on each of these three suspects, I can tell you exactly what I think."

"Great."

Ginette felt hopeful. These tough lady cops from the neighborhoods always knew the real deal.

Perez pointed to Dominick, jaw hanging like a Bassett hound.

"If he is the one ..."

Ginette stared at him with like. Suffering can be so endearing sometimes, especially to do-gooders. If the victim has a particular charisma, their attractiveness can corrupt someone like Ginette and make her feel heroic.

"If he is the killer," Perez continued, "he gets the chair. They won't have to shave off his hair. He doesn't have any."

Ginette knew that Dominick had heard Perez say this about him, but he didn't even touch his head. That's how flat he was. You could kick him in his shins and he wouldn't even yawn.

She ran her fingers through her own oily roots, and Nadine's voice flashed between her ears.

"If the killer is the redhead," Perez said, pointing at Fred, "he gets life. At least he's got a little zing. Juries like that."

Perez had this authority when she spoke. But it was illusory. Actually, the police were glorified doormen. They were servants.

"But if it's the old man who turns out to be responsible?" Perez nodded towards Jeff. He was overcome with a visible style of self-pity that seemed very familiar and habitual to the wearer. "I'd say that he'd get twenty–thirty, tops. Minus time off for good behavior, he'll be out in fourteen."

"That's life!" Jeff cried out from the cell.

"But not technically," Perez corrected. "And then there is the Socialite."

"Who's that?" Ginette asked, distracted by trying to figure out how to make Jeff take the blame.

"Harrison Bond."

"Harrison Bond?" Ginette froze. "What does he have to do with real life?"

"He did it!" Fred, Dom, and Jeff yelled out from behind bars.

Ginette stared at their three faces.

"He did it," they said again. "Harrison Bond is the killer."

In that moment, Ginette knew that they spoke the truth. She knew that if these three alienated men could simultaneously agree on something, it must be overwhelmingly true. *Oh God,* she thought, *Harrison Bond.* Ginette knew how powerful he was. She knew that he would never pay the consequences for anything he did wrong.

"Who did he kill?"

"A working girl. Claire Sanchez. From the Bronx."

Ginette's body froze so quickly that her nostrils dried up. *Oh no.* Of course he was guilty. He loved Claire Sanchez, the greatest motive for murder.

"How did she die?"

"The murderer stabbed the victim seventy-three times and cut out her heart."

Seventy-three times? Ginette knew what that meant. That meant love.

"Where is Mister Bond now?"

Perez scanned the Scan and read off the scanner. "He was released on a fifty-million dollar bond, posted by the East Hampton Writers' softball team."

"Perez, tell me," Ginette was deeply thinking, deeply planning, "if by some chance Mr. Bond was found guilty by a jury, what degree of punishment do you think he would receive?"

"If it's Casanova convicted of murdering some girl?" Perez laughed, flipping the tab on her vacuum-packed coffee from Japan. "He'd get an amazing book deal."

Ginette was exhausted, sludging home with low blood sugar. So what that her old boyfriend was a murderer. That fucking Claire deserved it. What a bitch! The way she said certain words was so fucking annoying. The way Claire swallowed was crime enough to justify being disemboweled. Many times, Ginette herself could have sliced Claire up with an axe. Ginette shed no tears and didn't care, ultimately, if Harrison walked. But it was her three little clients and their fate that consumed her. They were innocent and condescendable. Plus, it would hurt her promotion potential. If her clients were convicted of murder, she wouldn't get a raise. It was in the contract. They called it "merit pay."

More than ever her thoughts turned to Nadine. Now she had no future in counseling at all. If Nadine didn't call her back, she'd be ruined.

I'm gonna stalk that bitch, she thought. *I'm gonna fuck her.*

33. IMPERIALISM, THE HIGHEST FORM OF CAPITALISM

WHEN I FIRST heard about the Claire Sanchez murder trial, I was in my new office. I had done everything that Nadine asked for and gotten a better job writing marketing copy in THE MEDIA HUB. It wasn't that bad, and she had been right about everything. Once I put all my creativity into marketing, I was quickly promoted up the Byzantine escalator.

The Claire Sanchez murder was the lead story on the 2:45 news and then on the 2:55 news.

Not only was it a juicy passion killing that everyone could identify with, but it brought society's attention to the prison system and the courts. It was the first time since Sophinisba's election that someone who mattered had been arrested. There were editorials in all the tennis papers about the necessity of changing those systems immediately, so Harrison could have a trial that was appropriate to his way of life. A new reform movement came out of 1170 Park Avenue called LATS: Lifestyle Appropriate Trial and Sentencing. The members held meetings at the racquet club and got two tasks completed with one volley.

Since LATS and its sister group PECS (People Evaluate the Court System) were filled with all the people in the know, their plan went into action immediately. This brought even more attention to the case since it would be the first to be handled with this new sensibility. Everyone was very excited. Of all the new things that had happened, this was the newest. Rich people manipulating the system on their own behalf was as old as dust, but this time they said so. That really was brand-new. We all patted ourselves on the back for living in such an honest society.

"They're rebelling," Nadine said over toast. "Their egos can no longer stand earning money in the background while pretending that they're not in control. Now that everything they want is in place, the Richies are strutting their stuff. It's time for them to let us know who's the boss."

But Nadine was the only person I encountered who thought this way. Everybody else was enjoying the show thoroughly. In every office, bedroom, whorehouse, bar, and crack den, people were talking about the Sanchez murder. It had all the dimensions that folks love: Death, Sex, Fame. It didn't have any vague categories like "insider trading," which most people didn't totally get. No, this one was about BLOOD. This slaughter was easy and fun. We all loved it. We all followed it every second of the day for months and months.

I remember that the day of the actual trial, I was busy in the DNA room working on a helix. That's when we develop two publicity campaigns for two competing products, both of which we produce. When all the antitrust laws were recalled as a rider to Sophinisba's new policy making hairbrushes free for all, researchers determined that people needed and wanted the illusion of competition so they could get up in the morning. So, we—the Marketing Division of THE MEDIA HUB—were called upon to provide this service.

Product A was called *Weight Loss for Christians* by Darleen Mae Bodine, and Product B was called *Christian Weight Loss* by Archibald Smith, III. One product was for those consumers who identified themselves as white trash in certain kinds of targeted conversations. The other was for those who saw themselves as WASPS. This was complex advertising. Research surveys had shown that people try to outwit advertising by purposefully purchasing out of their own self-perceived niche. They know which ads are supposed to be for them, and it makes them feel excluded. Marketers call this *resistance*. For example, ads with black actors that were aimed at black people never showed in the same spheres of influence as the white-aimed ads. For this reason we employ the Hall of Mirrors strategy. People who really thought that they were white trash would not want to be so pegged. They had aspirations, after all. So they would buy the stuffier version because then they could imagine themselves to be thirty pounds thinner, and an all-brick Episcopal church came along with the fantasy. Real WASPS, on the other hand, had severe nostalgia for bacon, and when they imagined themselves losing ten pounds, they imagined eating slabs of it with blueberry pancakes on Sunday mornings in the country estate down home. Of course, when either of these niches purchased said object and then proceeded to not lose weight, they would reassess their selection and race to the Christian Diet shop to buy the other volume. Two turds with one bone.

Christian was my favorite department. All the queers and a couple of poets worked there. The most important word to use in the ad copy here was SATAN. Let's say you were marketing a hardcore, speed-metal Christian acid band. Well, you wanted to get a good juicy picture of Jesus on the cover, and then the copy would say "Easy Listening Is SATAN's Tool." And the nuke disc would be called "Jesus, Come Inside Me," and the band would be called "Virgin, Live." It was easy.

"Attention, attention," the red lights started flashing overhead. "All employees in the Gay, Lesbian, Bisexual, Transgender Focus Group, fiftieth floor please."

Obediently, I left my chair.

34. GETTING A TAN

HARRISON, OUT ON bail, lay on the beach at Southampton, preparing for his trial. He was preparing by working out, socializing, and getting some sun. When you're on trial, looks are all.

He knew why he had killed Claire. He was under pressure to produce a second book as masterful as the first, and she was aggravating his anxiety. So he had a trauma and tore out her organs. Harrison knew that it was messy but ultimately okay. This would blow over. Look at the sculptor Carl Andre. When a judge acquitted him of murdering his wife, Ana Mendieta, his prices went up. In this town, they can hate you today, but if they use you tomorrow, they'll love you. His tomorrow was just around the corner.

The outpouring of love and support from other guys and their sympathetic wives was incredible. Harrison had never felt so loved. Even other writers who had previously competed with him were loving and tender. They bought him drinks, they invited him to their beach houses. Every woman wanted to suck his cock out back on the beach at night behind some sand dunes. This murder charge was the best thing that had ever happened to him.

Harrison was so famous now. He was finally experiencing the cushion of fame that he had reached for all his life. He was now so famous that he was completely protected. No matter what he had ever done to anyone, he was beyond their reach. No matter what anyone knew about him, they were not famous enough to have a voice at the level of his. He never had to talk to or see anyone he didn't want to see. He was more alive than others. He was more important. His importance carried him on a conveyor belt of parties and privilege. He didn't have to live his own life. Fame was doing that for him.

And what about Claire? He could barely remember her, and why would he want to? That was then, and this was now. Move on!

That's why the New Spiritualists loved him. He was so capable of moving on that he could even move on from having taken another person's life. That was an amazing accomplishment, and they invited him to their parties, too. Veterans of the Iraqi War embraced his example. And former cabinet members of the Bush administration. Everyone wanted Harrison. Finally, he didn't have to feel at all.

The trial approached, but under the new LATS and PECS rules, it would be one of the greatest works of human display in the history of the very splayed American court system. It would create history. Harrison had already written a memoir about it and it hadn't even happened yet. Even though he had technically killed her, no one had to know that. Because, spiritually, he was innocent. Those ethnic weirdos Jeff, Dom, and Freddy, now those freaks were the real anti-socials. And that would become eminently clear. Harrison knew that he would win and they would lose. They would be blamed and, indirectly, they *were* responsible. They were creepy, and that was a crime in and of itself. If they had been more functional, he wouldn't have been under so much pressure to produce masterpieces for society, and what had happened wouldn't have occurred. It was their fault, and the trial would show this.

He'd written a novel about it, too, called *I Died*, told from the point of view of Claire's corpse. She explains the ways she goaded him into killing her, and how he is not really responsible. His plan was to publish this five years after the trial, just as his visiting celebrity status and grants and awards and movie versions had ended.

The publication of this book would open speculation all over again, creating a new round of parties.

He had always won, and he would always win. Harrison knew he was the champion.

35. ONE FOR ONE AND NONE FOR ALL

I GOT TO THE conference room, and there were all the other queers from work. There was that couple from Banking, George and George Henderson-Smith. And the pair from Graphics, Laurie and Laurie Nussbaum-Glukowski. Then there was Carolyn Steubanville-Woodson-Von Moschisker. (By the time she'd divorced Suzette Woodson, they'd already had four children: Waldo, Cornelius, Theodora, and Lucille. So shifting to Steubanville-Von Moschisker would have been awkward.) It had been years now since gay people were allowed to get married, the only hitch being the Monogamy Pledge. That was the compromise that The Human Universal Morality Battalion (THUMB), the gay lobbying group, had won in Congress. They attributed it all to the name change from The Human Universal Division. Throwing in the military image was crucial to winning in the southeast. Philip Morris, of which they were a department, suggested mandatory military service for all married gay couples to prove their loyalty. If they could go through basic training without telling anyone that they were married, the trust of their fellow Americans would be well deserved. That's progress.

Thank God for Democracy.

I had proposed to Nadine the minute gay marriage became legal, but she laughed. A few weeks later I asked her why.

"I'm old school," she said. "I'd rather live in sin."

Back at work we all knew that this queer beckoning from higher up had something to do with the trial. It was the center of the culture right now, and all resources had to be summoned. But how could the homos help them make money out of Claire Sanchez's ashes? There had to be a way.

36. THE TRUTH WILL IN

BACK IN THEIR cell, Jeff, Dom, and Fred knew they were doomed. I suppose that in some other kind of novel, they would use this opportunity to realize how much they had actually hurt each other, and would find a way toward the love. They would practice my own personal fantasy of redemption:

1. communication
2. negotiation
3. reconciliation
4. healing

Unfortunately, this was real life, so they just sat there missing every opportunity as each of them always had. Jeff missed Claire so much his teeth sank into his wrist. The other two just stared.

37. COKE IS IT

I WAS ANNOYED that day to be summoned away from my ongoing project of placing poems on cigarette packs. Poems were not selling and someone had to do something about it. Originally, the plan had been to sell ad space in poems. If there was a Coke on the landscape, the writer got a little royalty. But that still didn't solve the problem of no one wanting to buy the poem in the first place. So then we got the idea of slapping them on the packages right over the cancer warnings. Now, poems were part of daily life. All over the world, people sitting in bars were picking up their packs of Natural Slinkies or Big Bad Smokies and, in a moment of shyness or sudden quiet or any silence that revealed the profundity of human discomfort, any executive or logger or talent scout or drunk could look down on the table and see:

Daddy, daddy you bastard, I'm through.

Market research had selected that line as the most universal piece of poetry ever written. One that would translate into any culture and, at the same time, appear to be private and tender and touch a vulnerable spot. I was annoyed to be summoned away from my task because I also had to solve the problem of reintroducing products that had been developed for the homeless, which now had no one to buy them. Like body-sized Wash-n-Dri.

This wasn't the first time the gay subgroup had been beckoned by upstairs to solve a marketing dilemma. We had previously worked on the gay Gap campaign, developing two new divisions for virtual spinoff sites. There was ACT UP Gap and GMHC Gap. Each customer knew which one was for them. Then we came up with the "Audre Lorde Wore Khakis" campaign. But nothing was as successful as the "AIDS Is Over, So Live a Little" campaign for Brecht Pharmaceuticals. Riding on their notoriety for curing AIDS, the drug companies were now in the luxury vacation business, the beachwear business, and were running a national chain of No Fat restaurants and grocery stores. Of course, they still sold maintenance drugs to keep the formerly HIV positive in retroconversion. Sixteen pills, fourteen times a day, one hour after eating fat and two hours before eating sugar and two hours before eating no fat. If they ate fat when they weren't supposed to, or didn't eat fat when they were supposed to, they farted uncontrollably, which was a public recognition that they were Bad Boys, and didn't do everything their doctors told them. This had become a status symbol of rebellion, and there was now a chain of gay dance clubs called Farters where the Bad Boys would go.

As for everyone else with AIDS? Like who? I mean, the drugs were counter-indicated for methadone, birth control pills, and melanin.

Actually, that idea originated in my hub. It was thought of by Jay Friedman-Friedman, who'd died, suddenly, of a mysterious cause only a few months before. I wondered if it was suicide. He seemed so pale and skinny. He'd been depressed and had talked about quitting the business. But everyone tries to give up. There just is nothing else to do. People who can't make it in software become doctors. It's the lay of the land. That, or global investment. Go to Mexico and buy a duty-free family. I like copywriting. Replace words with words. An eye for an eye. That's competition on a level plane.

I sat and looked at the other gay marrieds, recalling the romance of visibility. It was so long ago, it couldn't be conveyed. Like nostalgia for Dacron or Dayton. Inexpressible. It was hot because you saw it. But what good is passion for its own sake? It haunts, internally. But Reputation goes on and on. So watch out.

The emotion of visibility was Corporate Downfall. Like what happened to Starbucks. Suddenly, there was a Starbucks where everything else used to be. It was too obvious. There was a Starbucks where the refrigerator store used to be, where the butcher, the florist, the Ukrainian/Italian restaurant, the wholesale grocer, the pierogi shop, the pawn shop, the stationary store, the hardware store, the thrift shop, the old bar, the prison, and three theaters used to be. The Korean delis were starting to seem eccentric and quaint. People resented the replacements and blamed all their problems on that fact. Visibility backfired.

Now that the franchises are gone, we don't have to see the Corporations bragging all over the streets. It's subtler. We only get it at home. Go outside if you want some privacy. It's public space, it belongs to you. Marketing only happens in the house.

"I've got it," Nadine said for the fourth time that day. "That's why everyone has to have a home. It's the law of the land. Homeless people don't make good consumers."

There she had it.

And for the first time I wondered if I shouldn't be going along with it all. Doing my job. Were other people thinking the same thoughts?

I'd gone out into public space that morning, on my way to work. I'd looked around to see if anyone else was worried.

Outside was so attractive. Bright orange, cheesy park benches like the old shag carpets of yore. The legendary plastic orange of motel chains, of Howard Johnson's. All kitsch classics, collectibles, and all for us. That's the color they painted the subway last week. Orange. Orange equals public space.

Orange = Public Space.

"Nadine," I'd asked, "from a design point of view, what does Orange mean?"

"Well," she sighed. "McDonald's discovered that orange makes people not want to stay too long. It keeps the public in circulation."

On the subway I saw a female scholar studying. Big hair, white jeans, legs akimbo. An all-important book. Good. They're back. It was an old-fashioned kind of tome. Some dead German. I saw two mothers on the subway. What were they discussing? Oh, yeah, how great their children are. An old man. An Albanian? He whispered to his daughter. Her skin was yellow with henna, just like the bleach job on the Italian lady across the aisle, the blonde black woman on the corner, and the Puerto Rican guy with a yellow watch that matched his hair. All blondes. In the orange. And it was all fine. Life went on.

38. THE GHOST WRITHER

"Now you all know why you're here," the Big Cheese told us
breezily. Smiling, sexy, lite. "I know that you are all familiar with the
murder trial coming up this Tuesday at nine p.m. Eastern Standard
Time. You've all seen the preview interview shows, the magazine
exposés, the Internet ads, and the Pre-Pre-Pay Views. However, we
need a tie-in slogan through which to market the trial accessories."
He was trim, white.

"As every American knows, there are two teams to choose from.
The public is being introduced to the new Freedom of Choice Legal
System, where they can choose between competing defendants, as
though they were shopping. It's more familiar that way."

His shoes were made of Sphinx™.

"Under the former system, choosing between innocent and
guilty was a negative choice. It was like going shopping or not going
shopping. We want people to go shopping no matter what, so we
have devised a new system whereby choosing between defendants
is like buying Tide or buying All. In the end, something is paid for.
I mean, someone has to pay."

He laughed, jingled his change.

"Now, according to our polls…"

I looked at the Big Cheese carefully. I had never seen him in
person before. He had a strange glow, like he was on TV. Then I
realized that he was wearing pancake makeup. I looked up and saw
that a tiny spotlight had been placed strategically over my shoulder
so that it could help him glow. Whenever he made eye contact with
any of us, a little light would shine our way. It made each of us feel
special, one at a time.

"Sixty-five percent of New Yorkers feel that the new legal system gives them more *flexibility* in their decision making. They feel more *secure* knowing that someone will be punished, and we know it creates double opportunities for product endorsement. Now, I think we're all clear that the bright young literary star from a good family with a gym body will be acquitted, and that the drug-abusing sociopaths will be convicted. So, given the odds, we've decided to prepare a book/movie/TV/digital/web/Teach-shirt tie-in on Bond that can be in homes from coast to coast fifteen seconds after the verdict is announced. However, we know that the post-Bond market will be flooded, principally by Bond himself. That's the problem with these artist types. They want to *express* themselves. So we need our end to have a unique focus."

Laurie Nussbaum-Glukowski raised her hand. She had long hair and pretended to be sexy. She pushed her breasts up so that her hook-word was *stacked*. She wore sexy midnight-blue silk pants. She flirted with all the men. Her clothes were more sexy than she was. I hated her instantly. But there is that thing about hate. If the hated would act a little bit differently, I would love them. It's a personality pattern. Therefore I sit panting with the expectation of the slight shift in behavior that will make everything new again. In this case, if she had been personal with me and had a private talk, instead of running away every time a man left the room, then I would have been her friend. I longed, at that moment, for the old days of the Secret Society when Nadine and I first fell in love, when gay girls sussed each other out right away and always found private moments to talk about what was really on their minds. The things that no one else could ever guess.

"Well, I think a homosexual angle on a case with no homosexual content would be fascinating," Laurie said sweetly. Ass-kisser.

"Just what I was thinking," Cheese smiled.

"A breakthrough that will call attention to the campaign itself, providing extra hyper-opportunities," Laurie offered.

"Well," coughed George Henderson-Smith, one of the hundred Harvard-educated black men working for the company. He was always sick from overwork, being in the Ivy League, black, upwardly-mobile, of middle-class origins, gay, married, HIV-positive, child of proud parents, collector of slave memorabilia, and member of country music niche study groups. "Fear and homosexuality go together like love and heterosexual marriage. According to yesterday's Home Poll, when forty-three percent of readers think of homosexuality, the first word they think of is "rich," and the second is "fear." Would it be too retro to recycle the homo-horror mode?"

That was it, the race was on. I started furiously keying in, but Nussbaum-Glukowski beat me to it, of course.

"I won!" she screamed, hitting the red bell. "*Het Cemetery.*"

Of course.

When heterosexuals kill each other, all the rest of them feel threatened. But to point out that they are heterosexuals—that was really threatening. They felt neutral, but now we said who they really are. It was a daring advertising tactic. Now they would be truly terrified to be targeted that way. Each of them would feel that they too, like Claire Sanchez, would have their organs sliced. And all because they're straight, straight, straight. Like Claire. WOW!

There was silence that came over the room. It was the kind of involuntary silence that accompanies the recognition of brilliance. A gift so profound that all petty competition is removed and you just gaze upon the other's work with awe and gratitude. Even though I had never read Stephen King and I hated Laurie Nussbaum-Glukowski, I couldn't hold back my admiration. And this would resonate broadly with our "AIDS Is Over, So Live a Little" campaign. Gay = Life. Straight = Death.

"*Het Cemetery*," she repeated, glowing. "Now, it's *your* turn."

39. IN JUSTICE

I WATCHED THE trial on my watch.

What was at stake? Our entire class system.

Nadine had seen through Sophinisba from the start. It didn't keep her from working for the mayor, but at least she knew what was right, even if she didn't do it. That put her ahead of most of the population.

I had noticed nothing. I had missed entirely that our mayor had not made things better. She just rearranged Capitalism so that it was easier to take. She made it more aesthetically pleasing, less visually oppressive, and threw us some bones.

But as the trial made clear, the same people were clearly in charge.

The same companies were making more of the same money, our same minds were being similarly enslaved. The same famous still had fame, and those with power remained powerful. It was all just prettier and a bit more fun.

Harrison claimed innocence. He had an explanation. He had walked in on these three monsters cleaning up after having murdered his love. Overcome with grief, he ran to her side and held her still-beating heart in his enormous hands. "Still-Beating Heart." That was his Defense Slogan.

Every guy who ran anything testified on his behalf, and Dom, Freddy, and Jeff had only each other.

So it was a done deal.

We'd all been framed.

It was a shocking revelation. And I wanted Nadine and I to unite in it. I wanted us to be alone together, like we used to be. That way we could go back to giving each other meaning in private, as all lesbians must.

But something had turned forever in her tiny heart. My stupidity, I suppose, made her love me less. Can that ever be undone? Where was she—my love? We needed to confess.

40. CONFESSSSSHUN

THE DAY HARRISON Bond was acquitted, he walked over to Glick's house. Not having any technology or devices, she didn't know anything about the trial. She was so out of it. She didn't even know that Spiro T. Agnew had died.

Glick was home, drawing, and making some onion juice. Assuming that Harrison was just a friendly visitor, she invited him in and lit up a Camel.

But then she realized that the man before her was in deep pain.

That's okay, she thought. She too was in pain. People shouldn't turn their backs. Glick was not afraid of other people's humanity. When they started to tell her something, she just sat back and listened.

It was all right to listen.

She didn't tell them, "shhhhh." She didn't tell them what she imagined she would do if she was in what she imagined to be their situation, and then insist that they make her fantasy of herself come true in their life. She didn't do that. She just listened.

She didn't tell them to "let go" or "move on" while screening their calls and not returning them, thereby causing more pain. She did not employ any of these dishonest and disrespectful ways to tell someone to shut up. That their life is worthless.

So when Harrison started telling her what happened, she just sipped her juice and listened.

"The day of her death, Claire was engaged with the insidious merging of longing and memory. Wanting the past," Harrison rhapsodized, baseball cap in hand. He was a novelist after all, so he could contextualize and terrorize other people's moments.

"People spoke to her over coffee, but she wished they were gone. She wished her next event was over. The next moment, over. The next. The next detached orgasm, embarrassingly complete. She came because she had to. Dishes dried, tub drained, TV flickering—oh no. She demanded isolation now so she could mourn her lost opportunities for peace."

Glick felt pretty relaxed.

"Claire looked for a bad book," Harrison said. "Hoping to not be in one. Hypocrite *lecteur*, have pity. It could happen to anybody who foolishly defends writers. *Ma semblable?* Oh, brother."

That last statement was pretty abstract, Glick noted appreciatively. She was trying to see the good in all people.

"Refusing to inhale, Claire prolonged the glow of her cigarette. Small moments of power. Can growing long toenails be a performance? The rain swayed, unheard. If she was British, her thoughts could possibly turn to the Queen from time to time. That's inevitable. That's their culture. But, alas, it was Diet Pepsi that crossed her heart."

Harrison looked at Glick.

"A knock came at her door," he said. "It was Harrison Bond."

He told Glick that the day in question had been Harrison's birthday. He had come over hoping for some kindness. Someone to say, "Happy Birthday, my friend. I love you. I'm glad you were born." And to give him a present.

Unfortunately, he came to the wrong house.

For Claire was busy rewriting the story of her life.

Somewhere, subconsciously, she knew that she had fucked Jeff over. She knew that cutting him off was cruel and detached, but she didn't care. Well, really, she didn't want to care, so she repressed it.

Somewhere she knew that she had deep, loving feelings for Harrison, but that made her feel terrified. She knew he would violate her. How did she know? Who cares? She didn't want to think about it.

As soon as he walked into her apartment, she felt loving feelings and deep desire. Therefore she hated him. She wanted to kill him. Everything was his fault. Everything.

"You are Satan," Claire said. "What you have done to me is worse than anything my father ever did to me."

"What did I do?" Harrison asked. It was his birthday.

"How could you do that to my life?"

"Do what?"

"I'm sorry that I ever trusted you. I will never, ever, speak to you again."

"Wait a minute," Harrison said. "What happened? It's my birthday. Can't you be nice?"

"You are desperately needy, you are suffocating me, demanding that I be nice. You are sick, sick, sick. Sick, sick, sick."

"Honey," Harrison said, both hurt and worried. "Honey? I know … I mean, I *do* know that your father sexually abused you. And I understand how that can make love threatening …"

"I hate you. I hate you. You are destroying my career. Everything about me is your fault, except that I am perfect. Well, FUCK YOU."

Harrison watched her splitting in front of him. He watched the person that he loved become a feral monster, possessed by the devil, lying to herself and the world every second. He watched her blaming him for all her pain—all of it, and pretending that the pleasure they had between them did not exist. It was the most dehumanizing, sinister kind of lie that any human can commit, to pretend away the love, the fun, the pleasure, and the kindness that you have received. It was awful.

"Did you kill her?" Glick asked.

"Yes," Harrison said.

"Shit," Glick said.

"Yeah," Harrison said.

"Do you want me to call the police?"

"It won't do any good," Harrison smiled for the first time in weeks.

"Why not?"

"Try it."

"Okay," said Glick. She picked up her receiver and dialed 911. "Nothing is happening."

"That's not their number anymore. Just say *police* into the phone."

"*Police*." She was connected immediately.

"Hello, officer?" Glick looked at Harrison intently as she spoke. "My name is Glick, g-l-i-c-k. I have a man here who is confessing to a murder. What? Yeah, I want to turn him in. His name is ..." She looked at him with raised eyebrows.

Harrison Bond, he mouthed.

"Harrison Bond. Yeah, okay." She put her hand on the mouth-piece. "They are running your name through the currency counter."

Harrison was happy.

"Yeah, I mean yes, officer. He's famous? No, I didn't know that. And who am I? Glick. Glick. G-L-I-C-K. Oh, you mean, WHO AM I? No one, I guess. Huh? What? His currency count is higher than mine so you won't take my report? You might get back to me? You might return my call? I thought that was only for getting tables in restaurants. Oh yeah, yeah, I did hear that there was some kind of new system, but I don't know what it is. Okay. So now, even reporting confessions require connections? Have you told this to the Catholic Church? Well, I think they have the right to know."

She hung up the phone.

"Why did you tell all this to me?"

"I knew that if you tried to turn me in, no one would call you back."

41. POSTER MORTEM

GLICK IS DEAD. A suicide.

Her note said:

Pattern and Design.

It was one thing being nobody alone in your apartment. But when people came over to tell you so, life was no longer livable. She'd given up.

Nadine and I watched her remnants lie scattered over the sidewalk, stepped on by traveling mailmen. Nadine broke down crying, and I watched her little shaking sadness, knowing that something new would come in its path. This gal wastes no time.

When Harrison Bond was released, I earned a bonus point. But it was when I was alone in my apartment, Nadine off in her studio, that I first saw Dominick's expression on the TV set. It was the expression of nostalgia for nothing. He'd never had a life, but now he missed it. I was caught. A tremor resonated from my past, all my former hopes. And I stared at the framed blank marriage certificate on our wall, longing for a quiet moment with my dearest one, when I could convince her to sign up. Something that was not possible and had never been possible. There were too many pressures.

Facing facts, and recalling the address of her compression chamber, I set off to pay my lover a visit for some mutual truth.

It was in a section of Manhattan I had never seen. It faces west over the diamond scope of sea. White spires of sailing ships rock obscenely without relent. Shifting their weight. It is a methodic movement, seemingly casual, but no human thereby engaged could escape without judgment. Disdain, likely enough. Perhaps confinement. Old white crow chewing passively atop its phallic peak.

The surface, of course, is thick, lurid, white. We long to see it emanating from the genitalia of our lady friends. Oh, that groan. Deeper than any tabletop word I've heard her utter. The sound of my lady's pleasure is sordid and therefore perfect, having reached the gravel depths that transcend every bit of etiquette. Thick, the sea, its weight the slick twixt algae and humanity.

It is summer now, but winter's cajole sits, undecided, on my lips. This new part of Manhattan must have a name. Avocadoville or Horse's Lane. Suzibelle Drive, Tequila Row. Lime and Salt Subdivision. Inferno. Har-ho.

In the breeze I remember, suddenly, my dead old friends. Some were sexy, some were sad. Together, a calm refrain of understanding, their vulgar deaths transcending fad.

I want to be a bowl of fruit on your lovely lap. Vagina Caverna is a kind, quiet place. My suddenly large fingers, yours braided white. One folded sky and its hidden head. Entire homes in Mexico are painted this color. Cavernous markets of colonial lust. Someplace between nectarine, red plum, and dust. Light cotton *shmattas* are ever so daring when artifice cannot conceal your appeal.

In this hidden part of the city, there is a twist around the cove. It's evening now and the soft mountain slums look out from the rock. Sallow lantern light. Yellow hand-dipped candles in clouds of glass. The streets are stairs. Top down from block to block. Carry your water for the best view. See your enemies before they see you. Around a dark corner in the soft yellow light, she paints with no windows. She just looks at her hands. She puts them in my pockets and then she lets go. This is just a few blocks away from Soho. Where men exchange lira twenty hours a day.

My friend the painter? I can imagine her, but I cannot see through her eyes. As a character she stumps me. Words are counter-indicated. Squirm on the meat-hook of verbal precision. I impose the spare room, the hue of light. I impose my own delight. But I cannot make the paintings on her wall.

"Look at me," I say.

I writhe, wide-eyed for her display. Scythe, sigh, task, tryst, width, gasp, grasp, twist. The spin within. Her horny body. The noose tightens as the evening speeds away.

I don't like men, I like you. In this neighborhood, my vagina is a two-way street. Children could conceivably come through, but I'd rather have that wine bottle propelled by your tender hands. If I was a gay man, I'd be dead. Penetration is very important to me. I want my lovers inside my body.

My vanity was calling, true. I wanted to be drawn by you. I'll see what you see. I'll be preserved for posterity. A map of your desire and your feelings about me.

And then I realized that Nadine would leave me. I, her catalyst for change, had become her old discarded self. Maybe later I'd get a thank you, but goodbye anyway. Then, someday, I'd happen to wander into a barro in her part of town.

FINISHED

SARAH SCHULMAN is the author of twelve books: the novels
*The Mere Future, The Child, Shimmer, Rat Bohemia, Empathy,
People In Trouble, After Delores, Girls Visions and Everything,*
and *The Sophie Horowitz Story,* the nonfiction works *Stagestruck:
Theater, AIDS and the Marketing of Gay America* and *My
American History: Lesbian and Gay Life During the Reagan/Bush
Years,* and the play *Carson McCullers.* She is co-director of the
ACT UP Oral History Project (*www.actuporalhistory.org*). Her
awards include the 2009 Kessler Prize for Sustained Contribution
to LGBT Studies, a Guggenheim Fellowship, Fulbright
Fellowship, two American Library Association Book Awards, and
she was a Finalist for the Prix de Rome. She lives in New York,
where she is a professor of English at City University of New York,
College of Staten Island and a fellow at the New York Institute of
the Humanities at NYU.

author photograph by Nayland Blake